X-1

EXPERIMENTAL FICTION PROJECT

The Smith : New York : 1976

Contents

THE SMITH: Letter to X-1	3
LESLIE WOOLF HEDLEY: Words About JB	5
HOWARD SCHWARTZ: An Assignment	16
W.D. WETHERELL: Chowder	18
ALVIN GREENBERG: Erotifictions	37
STUART DYBEK: Prayer	49
JERRY BUMPUS: The Love of Beasts	53
PETER BLIND: My Trip to Southern California On a Nine by Twelve Demo	67
RUTH MOON KEMPHER: The Yellow Book of Conversations	75
HUGH FOX: From Words From Xibala	88
IRENE MUSILLO MITCHELL: Scenes From the Thistledown Theatre	91
ARTHUR WINFIELD KNIGHT: The Finger	99
GIORGIO MANGANELLI: Insert: On Saying Goodbye Translated by W.S. DI PIERO	106
EDWARD MARCOTTE: The Marginalist	114
BEV JAFEK: Conversations With the Minotaur	117
SAMANTHA POMERANCE: We Only Want You To Be Happy Janet	141
OPAL L. NATIONS: The Woman Beautiful	143
DICK HIGGINS: Women, Like Horses	147
CHARLIE SISE: I Had Never Noticed	151
MIKE FIORELLA: With But One Simple Step	178
STUART S. PETERSFREUND: Morning Fragment With Dogs	184
SAL YOUNG: Bourn	187
ALLAN LUKS: Bus	199
GARY LIVINGSTON: Hunt	202
STANLEY NELSON: It was	205
HARRY SMITH: The Universe is Not for Sale	223
Contributors' Notes	back inside cover

cover by George Mattingly

Copyright © 1976 by The Generalist Association, Inc. All rights reserved. First edition, June 1976. Published by The Smith, 5 Beekman St., NYC 10038.

Library of Congress Catalog Card Number 76-20256.

ISBN 0-912292-41-5

Editors for this project: Harry Smith, general; Tom Tolnay, managing; Anne C. Heller, coordinating.

Dear Reader,

We embarked on X-1 without preconceptions. We simply publicized our intentions, curious as to the experimental lines that would emerge. In the process of discovery, we applied no arbitrary criteria to test the works. Rather, we judged in response to the evocative charge carried to us, our fascination with the design, its capacity to extend our limits.

If we'd had to guess, we'd have predicted more direct probes into technik mindsets. But mostly these writers treat our technocracy indirectly, through symbolism as in W.B. Wetherell's "Chowder" or in such allegorical mindscapes as Edward Marcotte's "The Marginalist" or superreal urbscapes as in Peter Blind's "Trip to Southern California on a Nine by Twelve Demo."

We have excluded performable plays from this collection, as we accommodate them in our ongoing experimental theatre anthology. Still Bev Jafek's "Conversations with The Minotaur" is here "on a plane somewhere between psychodrama and guerilla theatre."

Likewise, we have not sought poems with fictional elements, as we publish these in
[MORE]

the main series of our literary magazine. The one exception is Opal Nations' "The Woman Beautiful," where the verse form itself is part of the fictional intent.

A few X-1 writers -- Jerry Bumpus, Dick Higgins, Alvin Greenberg, Leslie Woolf Hedley -- are well-known on the avant garde, though little-known elsewhere. For others, X-1 is the vehicle for their first published fiction.

The collection proceeds from works which are experimental only in thematic development to fictions which break the spatial conventions of prose. Stanley Nelson's prose, for instance, partakes of techniques originating in projective poetry. The traditional novel, after all, is but a degenerate form of epic, and in the current revitalization of fiction, the traditional distinctions between poetry & prose are dissolving in the creation of new forms.

June 15, 1976

Words About JB

LESLIE WOOLF HEDLEY

JB was a professed champion of Grand Causes.
his biographer sits there perhaps with microscopic intentions and I wonder about those Grand Causes which made up the fount of JB's radical reputation a reputation he cultivated and nurtured

"He must have been a dynamic person," the biographer placed his official words together for my convenience. They were hors d'ouvre for me to nibble. "You knew him for several years."

"Yes, I knew JB when he lived here," I answered. "After he left we drifted apart

JB drifted among Grand Causes how could he be interested in anything or anyone but his Grand Cause of the moment I received occasional letters bulletins really about JB from JB self-advertisements but this guy opposite me may not want to know that all-too-human behavior of a newly dead hero don't rock that chapter in my book he's probably thinking that's why he's giving me the lead words so I mustn't disturb illusions humans are easily frightened when you tell them $1 + 1$ doesn't always $=$ exactly 2 that's a surface equation why not rather say that sometimes this kind of $1+$ that kind *of 1 = a transitory 2 but this fellow wants me to jump into a ready pool of selective memories and come out holding clean slogans issues responses epigrammatic sayings u goddamned neat catalog to sell JB*

because of distance," I explained. "He was working on the East coast and I was here on the West coast. You understand?" Did he?

He nodded.

I waited for his Book-Of-The-Month-Club-brain to click.

"We were speaking of JB's dynamic personality," he said.

dynamic ah that's the word this dynamic biographer gives me to chew a dynamic word and yes one might say JB was dynamic in his robust Whitman-Hemingway manner his toucan nose his driving hard dedication to the Grand Cause of himself there's nothing unusual about that ego drive businessmen artists generals politicians athletes may be dynamic but is it a virtue or a vice I don't know it becomes a game of metaphor

"JB had a certain presence," I limned. "He was an attractive man with a good voice. JB also had poise and some height. This helped give him what some people called an aura."

"Stage presence? That's good."

"Yes,

how he loved the stage and how easily JB would utilize his surroundings vibrations shades nuances whatever he could sense and played with it carefully balancing paradoxical positions it amused him to be on that stage almost any stage I recall a conversation JB venting bitterness that he wasn't in-

vited to speak in this city and how he condemned our cultural gangsters until suddenly he was invited to speak and they no longer were gangsters but fine perceptive people of taste having exhibited this taste inviting JB he could move as quickly as that as long as his macroego was perpetually fed he offered sublime rationalizations

JB could handle himself in front of students and the intellectual public," I said.

"I was thinking especially," the biographer of JB moved restlessly in his chair, "of his leadership ability. In particular, when you first met him, during those days of the Grand Cause. JB was elected Chairman. This was a major revolutionary step for a man with the family background of JB," he emphasized.

I agreed. "Yes." Then I supplied my own emphasis. "It was JB's first collective effort."

no one would serve as Chairman I was too young inexperienced it was unfashionable being young then and the older ones were afraid of losing job status car home wife sabbatical Guggenheim Ford cash friends who knows I had just got out of the army happy to be alive but the others had mixed opinions they looked around for someone of pure background noncontroversial solid respectability were their very words so we then asked JB who hadn't even bothered to attend our early meetings or expressed any radical sentiments having previously considered such ideas as the unhappy ravings of unfortunate intellectuals and JB was flattered perhaps never thinking of possible dire consequences enjoying the thrill of an easily won leadership the chosen man as it were and it was an accident a tactical ploy using his mushrooming ego to serve our (or so we thought) Grand Cause and JB made a good Chairman because he loved being center of attention he handled press conferences and made certain he employed that word I I I I repeatedly the Grand Cause soon lost its collective purpose becoming a secondary issue buried under countless I I I I JB made the Grand Cause eponymous

The writer continued our duolog. "The risk he took was great."

I smiled. "The risk we all took was either great or small, depending on how far down we might fall." Poetry and truth in one sentence.

He ignored that. "I mean that JB

old JB I'm sorry you're dead and I hope someone will be sorry when I'm dead you were a nice guy in your way and I regret being placed in this position I'm sitting here searching out the freckles and rugosities of your former life in this city it all seems unnecessary and ominous because humans devour and shit out histories and it doesn't matter to 99.9% of this silly hive that Beethoven Schubert Joyce Lorca Van Gogh hundreds of painfully authentic geniuses are dead or even that they once lived

was very much part of American history. He was considered—"

"I'm aware of how media considered JB after the Grand Cause," I interjected. "I suggest only that you don't exaggerate

JB had gambled he could afford to gamble he relished an awed public the kind of elementary danger which was always

slightly Hollywoodian with JB adroitly dressing the part in blue levis and boots laying aside his London suits ties shirts because JB risked becoming a cause celebre and this was mixed up in his professed intentions sincere intentions I do say sincere goddamnit but it was stirred with natural secret impulses a product of his powerful family opportunitas clara who can say for sure but it was plainly visible with tv cameras lights reporters basking JB and the knowledge I say knowledge that he had plenty of Blue Chip Stocks tucked away accumulated by his family while the rest of us had nothing

the risk he took. You see, those of us on the committee never thought of the risk, but only of the Grand Cause. We discovered the risk after-the-fact."

"After you were all fired from the university?" he asked with an official smile.

"That's right. Many of us were *echt*-radicals. We only knew theory and books. During that crisis period JB represented us very well. He was more . . . well, expedient." What I laid out for him dissipated somewhere between the tip of my tongue and his ears.

"But I mean," the man leaned forward, "JB was older

richer say richer more secure comfortable had a room with a view several rooms with excellent views my mind can't help play counterpoint

and therefore had more to lose

had everything to gain mister he couldn't lose but we're now playing the game of your cup is half full and my cup is half empty

than the rest of your committee," he said with a touch of pique.

no we lost our jobs everything JB became known as the voice of our Grand Cause while we were seeking work whatever we could get JB settled on a family estate and wrote his memoirs a now famous book and he carefully passed over all our names as though we had been sedate shadows under his oak yes that did hurt our pride our tarnished beaten bitter salted pretzel souls our unemployed tender skins because we were so easily shrugged aside overlooked in that hectic period while JB traveled spoke traveled spoke the symbol of our lost battle now the only symbol of our unremembered Grand Cause

I knew this writer wouldn't grasp any of this. I couldn't fault him for not understanding. No one should ever understand too quickly. "Yes," I sighed.

"Didn't you meet his son? I believe he came out here to help JB during that crisis?"

"Briefly. JB's son was teaching in one of those cute New England schools. He came for a quick visit one summer—that hot summer, as the newspapers called it," I said. "We just

a microcephalic poet with enormous beard whose still more enormous lack of talent was being stupendously rewarded by certain colleges he spent his time sniffing bottoms of adolescent boys and borrowed money from JB to buy a sportscar

said hello. We certainly didn't require his assistance. Frankly, what we needed was a good lawyer."

He shuffled notes. "Hmm."

this noted bestselling biographer wanted something more exotic than my dry reminder that we needed a lawyer it doesn't mean anything he can't hang his biographical hat on that hook because he never needed a lawyer

"But," he then wondered, "his son coming out here at that crucial time, that precise danger point, as it were, does certainly reflect an intimacy and warmth between JB and his son.

warmth another word to be added after dynamic JB and son hadn't seen each other for years JB didn't care for his son's peculiar sexual proclivities and JB junior was always trying to borrow more money from dear old daddy the rich have heirs not children warmth no that never entered except in exchanges of temperament his son being interviewed by the city press on his arrival having come he said to aid his august father's Grand Cause hirsute chin thrust into the air but JB felt his son might borrow more than money perhaps steal public focus away from JB well let's say that JB had a warm handshake

Doesn't it?"

I said nothing, hiding my silence, lighting a cigar.

"It's this essential warmth in JB's nature that I find so vital in his writings," the biographer explained. "It was this facet of his personality which urged him to help others.

why would JB help others anyone at all such an energy

output was alien to him not because he was mean but because JB was a talker not a listener incapable of anything outside of himself including wife children friends associates strangers because nothing existed outside himself unless as a background to himself JB fancied himself a moralist but that doesn't indicate he was humane

Not only during the Grand Cause but throughout his life. That, to me," the man said, "is the glue holding together my biography of JB. His sense of human sympathy

more words JB would discreetly smile sulkily at another person's disaster by reducing it immediately to an imagined trivia paranoia he had a way of folding together his broad face prominent nose into a slightly mocking patronizing package not cruel no but he diminished everyone's agony to insignificant deliquescence not cruel no but when you caught a sharp glint of it from JB's bright eyes you recognized that you didn't matter at all and his protective ego coating his immunity a lifetime of family immunity so lesser beings around him he dismissed facially with a smile forever it was simple if JB needed you he tolerated you if he no longer needed you you vanished maybe that's pragmatic sympathy a quid pro quo *deal a symbiosis from a distance it appears noble sweet brave what one professes and what one is ah two separate things that's the crux of it but this mustn't be allowed to soil JB's established reputation his solid gold obituary*

for the common man."

I never doubted JB was in love with the public the common man as this guy has it as long as their hands applauded him he loved the common man in the same manner a suction tube loves a blood donor for towards the end JB had started to believe he was John Brown they had the same initials

"Yes," I answered.

"During the latter part of JB's life," my interviewer's tone was now marvelously soft, "he became increasingly oriented toward religion. You knew that?"

"I think so."

"Did he ever discuss this religiosity with you?"

I chewed on a lozenge of memory and raised my shoulders. "I can't recall

holy words well it's too good a business to leave out JB knew he made an occasional blend of Radicalism & Religion bringing God into his talks certain that God would allay any suspicion of dangerous radicalism when ever he felt it advantageous sharing his podium 50/50 with God the older people and more mystical youth loving it JB sometimes wore a homespun old monk's robe and a crucifix hanging from his heavy neck O charisma

that JB ever made any point of it."

"You're smiling," he aimed his pen. "A happy recollection about JB cross your mind?"

"You might say that."

it flashed why is it this light maieutical biographer needs to make JB into a hero why all the fuss fencing around our rusted Grand Cause and I saw it saw behind the words JB had been part of that rugged individualism of American mythology-history part of our heritage Carnegie-Ford-Rockefeller-

Vanderbilt-DuPont part of that stock and breeding a safe hero for young Americans a perverse and almost delicious somersault of logic for now the recrudescent Tom Paines-Jeffersons-Robespierres-Marxs-Lenins of this society were employed as executives brokers human engineers bankers professors lawyers physicists computer specialists boys from good home good family all under the umbrella of a new American techno-state because our leaders were learning to keep future revolutionaries gainfully employed for revolutions now would take place at that higher economic executive level leaving an imaginary radical kinesthesia for the gullible masses and JB fit their image they O that magical they preferred it made sense they wanted JB to be that purified respectable inspiration that perfect radical who would never do a single radical act that's why this biography that's why this smooth layer of coldcream interview because they knew that JB was pragmatic putty molded by them under kleig lights he was the perfectly designed artificial revolutionary hero for boys and girls

I studied my exhaled smoke go up like illusion. The hell with it. Life is a concatenation of minute betrayals of Grand Causes. No one can refute myths.

no one defeats advertising in America truth is only for those with moral strength to withstand pain knowing every published truth has some kind of covert lie clinging to it as it passes from mind to mind mouth to mouth hand to hand no not mine I won't be a dead hero again again again shouting to the world because the world doesn't want to listen doesn't have to listen doesn't even need to listen to more words words

WORDS ABOUT J.B.

because why should anyone believe me when now all belief is suspended between one's ability to pay the rent so it's impossible lies within lies and wheels within wheels and off we go words diminish words

"JB," I told him, "was one of the most courageous men in this country. He was the conscience of his generation."

An Assignment

HOWARD SCHWARTZ

I was given an assignment by Nixon to move a cage without looking inside it. I disobeyed the order and lifted the cover off the cage, which contained a huge, radioactive turtle, taken from one side of our island. I knew this meant that side had been contaminated, and that other sides were endangered, eventually the whole island, and I conferred with several friends to decide what step we should take.

Two weeks later, on the eve of a ceremony of dedication, there was all sorts of evidence that things had been thrown out of order. A father had held back the eggs he must surrender; a child had taken a dedicated ring apart and sold it for a toy; and another child was using a medical tool as a toy, with subsequent danger. And on the day of the dedication I was made to ride in a car that carried a primitive animal. The others did not consider it dangerous, but when it snapped at me I kicked back and broke its beak, and this upset everyone and angered the animal, who then made a real effort to bite me and nearly succeeded.

That night, when I looked out the upstairs window, I saw a shadow cast outside the front door. And when I leaned over the stairway I saw Nixon standing alone, peering up to the rooms above and reporting my dream to those below. When I demanded an explanation he backed off towards one of many halls, transformed himself into a limping cat that slid beneath a dresser, and would not be moved. Just then a bird started to shriek, and with certainty I moved to break the spell, tossing it from the window with the command, *Vulture, explain your wings!*

Chowder

W. D. WETHERELL

There was a hammock on the corner of the sundeck closest to the sea. Troubled all day by a vague urge toward weightlessness, Atlas had taken to it early, completely ruining what Jack insisted on calling "the last barbecue" for the others. He wasn't feeling particularly bad about it—just enough remorse to break the ice. As he listened to the sound the sand made spilling from Amy's sneakers onto the dry cedar of the deck it occurred to him that despite it all a lot of terrible things had happened.

"Hiroshima Nagasaki," he said off the top of his head, and immediately a sharp pain billowed in and out between his three highest ribs.

Down through the years a lot had happened. Not that it mattered anymore, of course. Tangier had already taken the twins across and was due back for the rest of them by midnight. The furniture that was left was piled on the beach just above a line Atlas had drawn with the bottom of the umbrella to show them where the evening tide would come. So it was foolish, but it was one of the rules . . . No Radios, No Newspapers, No Sand In Your Shoes Beyond The Sundeck.

"I want to apologize for throwing the shell at you," she said at last, but stiffly, in the formal tone that had crept between them in the day and a half since she had let the guitar escape.

"Hiroshima Nagasaki," he said again, with a trace of irritation in the voice this time. "Dresden."

But at least it gave her time to think. She was still out of breath from running up the beach ahead of the others. Kathy had made a detour to the furniture, Jack was carefully spreading the leftover briquettes along the base of the house.

"The last sunset!" he yelled when he saw her watching him. He pointed back over his shoulder.

It was a brown one, not the kind they preferred there in September, but fast, as if going down to spare them any nostalgia. She watched it in the dutiful way she took everything on Axehold, the same way she rubbed the suntan lotion across the twins' shoulders when they came out from a swim, the same way she took out the guitar after she finished wiping the lotion off her hands. She wanted to give it up after the twins were born, but Atlas wouldn't let her. It makes it easier for me, he said, and he would lay pressed into the sand with the tense, hunched-up sort of acceptance people working out with weights sometimes have until she started to play. Her fingers were stiff from being out in the sun all summer, her voice couldn't possibly have reminded him of what it sounded like when they first met, but she could see it relaxed him and anyway it was demanded of her—just as he demanded grace of Jack and beauty of Kathy—in return for his support.

"I think we should talk before they come up."

"Andersonville."

The sag in the hammock chopped back and forth once like a grimace, then swung to a stop. He was all but buried in paisley folds front and rear—she couldn't see his face or tell which end was which in the dark and she was almost to the hammock before she remembered they weren't alone. The girl had stayed behind, too . . . against the wall as motionless as ever, long tan legs slightly apart in the remaining light, disappearing into white shorts, then shadows. She wasn't sure. She might have moved a bit closer to the hammock since they had left.

"State capitols," she said apologetically. "They relax him."

The girl said nothing. She was definitely closer to the hammock than she had been before.

"Treblinka," Atlas said. "Dachau."

"Wyoming!"

Kathy ran upstairs from the beach, her hair still wet from what Jack was calling the last swim.

"I never can remember it."

She had left the top half of her bathing suit on the beach and talking so fast seemed in her the same modest gesture a woman with less pride would have used to cover herself with her hands. It was an appeal . . . Amy understood that, even sympathized with her. But she couldn't help feeling it was breaking another of their rules all the same. They decided to ask Jack when he came up.

"Cheyenne," he said knowledgeably, wiping the charcoal off in black curls down his chest. "You missed some great chicken, Al!"

"Kentucky? South Dakota?" Kathy asked, in the same fast, insistant way.

"Frankfort. I thought it was great anyway."

"South Dakota?"

"Bismark. What gives?"

"Are you sure?"

"Louisville then. I don't. . . . Why?"

"Don't be such an ass, Jack," she said automatically, in a tone she had obviously been saving all day. "We've got to do something."

Of course that was just it. Nothing could be done. They had already moved the house four times in the past two years. Twenty-five feet of beach had gone in the spring tides, another fifteen in the last storm. There was nowhere left to go.

"He won't be back for hours yet. We just can't sit here dissolving."

"Okay, okay," Jack said, making a little questioning motion with his head toward the hammock. Kathy looked away. Amy shook her head. He had sat down next to her, then moved closer when Kathy turned, keeping his hand on her knee until she turned back again, responding—Amy assumed—to Kathy's missing bra, which in turn seemed connected to the twins being gone, or a last pathetic attempt to please Atlas.

"Okay, so what about West Virginia?"

"For God's sake, not tonight," Kathy said. "I know Al doesn't mind and I suppose you don't either by now Amy, but after ten years.... Oh, hell," she whispered, "Just not tonight."

"Wounded Knee. My Lai...."

"Wheeling," Sue said quickly. "Wheeling.... He's not serious, Kathy."

"I don't care if he is or not. It's not right. Not tonight. Any anyway it's Charleston."

There was nothing they could talk about safely. To the east was a wildlife refuge, populated by gulls who flew there to escape the city for a couple of weeks each summer.... On humid days they rose together to feed off the trailings of jets that flushed down the horizon right to left, using Axehold as a sight on the mainland just as the seabirds did flying south in the fall. Directly behind was the old golf club. Their latest move had nestled them into the dogleg on the fifteenth fairway and golfers had taken to ricochetting their drives off the twins' side of the house to kick past the rough on the left. Jack gave the greenskeeper fifty dollars to rule them out of bounds, but the course itself was threatened now—it had gone from a par 74 to 66 in the last three months, losing eight strokes to ocean—and when the club's surviving board of directors decided to build a seawall to save the fifteenth it had gone up just behind the house, cutting them off from the road and any kind of salvation.

It was tacitly understood that Atlas was suffering the most. He had known Axehold before any of them, back in the half-legendary days when beauty itself seemed requisite for landing there. His mother had been imported from the city to dance at the old casino. His father was a shellfisherman, the last of his race. . . . Atlas hadn't left the island for the first twenty years of his life and when he did leave he carried Axehold's immunity with him—his chest and shoulders were heavy with it, broad and full—an inheritance of beauty and strength that bore him through a world most islanders, island-raised, have no resistance to.

Amy used to love hearing Kathy tell how they had first met him . . . the young giant lost in the city, walking blindly into the grill of their Thunderbird one snowy night on Lexington Avenue. "Dammit, you killed him!" Jack had yelled, but when they got out they saw he only had a slight cut on his arm—he was staring at the blood like he didn't know what it was. They took him back to their apartment and bandaged it for him with the mixture of condescension and awe that in various combinations marked their attitude toward him from then on. Sometime during the night he told them about Axehold. . . . Their adoption was complete.

Only in March did he ever stagger, only when he had been gone too long, so they would open the summer house in April, two months before anyone else, and you could see his knees almost buckle in gratitude the minute he walked ashore.

It was a strength they thought nothing could ever touch. One summer the state park commission decided to build a bridge from the mainland but they had run out of money before it was through. You could still see it across the bay, a foreshortened steel blueness jutting out from the coast toward Axehold in a strange rigid gesture of longing. Every so often a car would blunder its way through the barrier of a dark, drunken night and go off the end, flying into the water as if to achieve Axehold in one desperate vault. There, Atlas had once said, pointing to the bridge, is the threat where the danger will come and so when years went by and the cars came no closer, they naturally assumed there was no danger at all.

Fingers of the sea had stolen in on each of the five nights since Labor Day, making off with the twins' croquet set on Monday, the spare hibachi on Tuesday. Wednesday the boathouse had gone, Thursday the beach chairs. On Friday, the day it came and took the guitar, Atlas signaled Tangier to come.

"Dallas. Stanleyville...."

The voice from the hammock seemed to be getting softer, but increasingly slurred, punctuated with throaty burps that could have been either hiccups or recoils from syllables that seemed to flow faster and faster over the sides.

Losing the guitar had been her fault. It was careless of her to leave it so close in the first place and even then she probably could have saved it. But she just stood there watching it float serenely away, the twins' blue pail bobbing up and down against its neck like a buoy. When Jack saw all of them watching without doing anything, he threw off his robe and ran in after it, diving through the first waves with the joyous, seal-like nonchalance he had always had at his best.

"He's got it!" Kathy yelled.

But the sea had changed. He underestimated it . . . they saw him turn back a hundred yards out emptyhanded, then they lost him in the dark green folds. It seemed like an hour went by. Kathy was trying to get up the courage to ask Atlas to go in after him when a wave smaller than the rest rolled him out onto the beach with a kind of disdainful deliverance, sparing him only enough strength to crawl beyond the edge of the surf and collapse. Kathy ran to him but he pushed her away and staggered off down the sand. . . . All this time Atlas had been lying on his blanket, one hand propped beneath his head, watching without a sound.

Jack got up for some more ice. Amy hadn't realized how dark it had become—when Jack opened the refrigerator the light from the freezer shot across the deck to the hammock. "Calcutta, Eboli . . ." the voice said and then the door slammed shut, leaving them in blackness again. Jack felt his way over and dropped an ice cube into each of their drinks, then fixed one for Atlas and left it on the deck near the hammock, but far enough away so he'd have to get out if he wanted it.

"The last ice cubes," Jack said, throwing the extras over the side. "Happy last ice cubes."

"Will you please stop calling them the last. Call them penultimate, final, ultimo, but. . . . Oh, anyway. It's not the last anything. You make this sound like a goddamn wake."

"Here it is. And I'll tell you why."

He was off again. On how much it had cost them to buy the place in '65. On how much the taxes were plus the interest on the mortgage, divided by the number of weeks they spent up there, divided by the number of waves each hour, or how much each wave had cost them or was costing them or would cost them if they let it take the house. He kept saying it was simple but the more he said it the more complicated it seemed. Amy soon lost track of what he was talking about.

She was worried about the twins. She didn't know they were taking them off so early and she had gone up the beach by herself, searching for shells to work with over the winter. When she turned to go back Tangier's boat was already anchored off the beach. Atlas had taken the twins under either arm and was wading out to him. . . . She could see them kicking their legs against his powerful, suntanned back in delight, and she could imagine their screams of pleasure. And she thought she had never seen him look so strong. . . . But something, the heedless way Atlas marched into the sea, the fact they were leaving without saying goodbye, had terrified her. It was too far to run; she tried to yell but the sound was soaked up by the sand before it could cross the beach. Atlas was almost over his head by the time he reached Tangier's boat; he hoisted the twins onto his shoulders and lifted them over the gunwale into two dark receptive hands that pulled them greedily out of sight behind the cabin. It was then she had thrown the shell, just as he turned around and lifted his eyes toward where she stood helplessly on the beach.

"Sodom. Auschwitz."

"Just a second, just a second," Kathy yelled, doing her best to sound cheerful. "It's killing me. . . . Uh, Delaware, right?"

Jack made a sarcastic little cough. Kathy ignored him, then sulked. Amy suggested cards.

"Tangier took them yesterday with the beach towels. Why I don't know. I thought I told you to save them."

Kathy was looking at the girl. She had belonged to one of the families they had rented the place to back in June when they were still naive enough to think they could save it. She stayed on when they reclaimed the place in August, turning up for dinner the first night as if it was the most natural thing in the world. Kathy tried to get rid of her, but Jack said something to Atlas and she had stayed on as a babysitter for the twins, though she seemed more of a companion, one of them, than anything else. . . . She seemed wholly dedicated to the sun.

"Did you?"

There hadn't been room for her in the boat. With the twins gone she had kept to herself in the corner.

"Little Miss Innocence isn't talking."

"Knock it off, Kathy. The kid isn't to blame. I know how

you feel. I don't want to go back either. None of us do. It's not her fault they don't give you flood damage in this goddamn state."

He would have been off on another tirade if it hadn't been for Atlas who had suddenly begun burping out the names uncontrollably, one right after the other in groups of threes, separated by great belches of air that seemed to shake the entire deck. Jack giggled. Kathy seemed uncomfortable. Amy got up to look for some candles. None of them had ever seen him that human.

"Guerni what?" Kathy asked. Then, a minute later, "I wish he'd stop it."

"Where did he learn all those?"

"I don't know. Showing off I guess."

"Not from me. It's terrible but that's the way things are. We'll buy a place somewhere else."

"What am I going to tell the twins?"

"Nothing. Kids take things in their stride."

"World War Two battles," Jack said, in the same knowing way he had told them about Cheyenne. "Dunkirk, Pearl Harbor."

"It's because he hasn't had anything to eat," Amy said. "Not since breakfast."

"I thought we were playing state capitals?"

"Not since last night."

"Well, whatever. It's better than nothing."

But they ran out of battles early. Amy couldn't remember any except D-Day, Kathy got bored, Jack kept cheating with World War One . . . he had a great uncle who was emasculated at Vimy Ridge. Behind them in the hammock the voice was louder, but at least the burping had stopped. He seemed reciting them by rote now, in the mechanical style of a conductor calling off the stations on a suburban railroad.

Kathy went over to the hammock. It was the only thing left

to save and she wanted to remind Atlas to bring it along when the time came.

"Kathy," the voice called. "Attica...."

"I know, I know," she whispered, in the gentle way she always had with him. "But don't forget it all the same."

No response. When she reached down half-playfully to pull the fold of cloth off his face there was a violent jerk and the hammock almost swung off the hooks that held it to the rail. It took a painful thousand-year burst of noise, from Salamis to Salem, before the hammock stopped swinging and the voice resumed its monotonous drone.

"Are you okay? Hey, is he okay?"

"He's hungry," Amy said. "I told you."

There was still some chicken left. They put it on a plate near the drink with a candle and waited to see what would happen. Jack had been going through the other rooms making sure they had everything. He came back with a boxful of old comic books, a bathing cap and a black, derringer-shaped water pistol.

"For self-defense," he explained, sticking the pistol into the waistband of trunks. "Hey Kathy, you want this cap?"

"What color is it?"

"Red. Ugly red. Puerto Rican red."

It wasn't hers. Amy didn't recognize it either so they decided to add it to the briquettes with the comics.

"You've been in the sack long enough, Al. How's about a hand with these?"

There was no answer.

"I don't think he wants to," Amy said. She was mad at herself for sounding so timid. "I mean I don't think he should. He's done enough. He deserves to relax now."

"Yeah, well.... He better not relax when the time comes. And that reminds me." He waited until he was sure they were listening. "When the time does come I want all of us to take off our suits."

Kathy groaned. Jack went on as if he hadn't heard her.

"That way it'll seem like we were asleep when it broke out. Just barely escaped with our lives. Hell, we've all seen enough of each other anyway."

"You're so unbelievably obnoxious when you're taking charge."

"Anyway," Jack said, with less conviction, "I think it's a good idea."

"Vimy Ridge! All you ever talk about is old Uncle Ted losing his at Vimy Ridge!"

"Vimy Ridge," Jack said again, defensively this time.

"Vimy Ridge," Amy said, trying not to laugh. It had such a ridiculously safe sound.

"Don't you start too, Amy. I think it's a good idea, period. Kathy's halfway there anyway so who's complaining."

He started down the ramp with the comics, then changed his mind and began scaling them over the side one by one . . . they caught the breeze and hovered open like huge bats before swooping away. In the dark you could see light horizontal strips of burnt yellow where the decking had split apart enough to reveal the beach. The furniture they were leaving behind had slid into the kitchen. The bedrooms had sunk into the sand. The whole house lay tipped toward the sea, breaking up in the same maritime style they had always tried for . . . like a ship bow down on a reef.

"The last piss," Jack yelled. "Be right back."

From where they sat on the edge of the deck you could see nothing but ocean, a white breaking line of surf. A few steps backwards, uphill, you could see over this toward the other side of the bay, the red, blue and green lights that seemed to swarm about the horizon summer-long and—on nights as dark as this one—shake themselves above it into stars. Amy had been watching them for ten years. Atlas taught her how to pick out the steady white shades of the lighthouse and the blinking red, red, red of the radio beacon near the ferry landing, but the lights further out in the bay had always refused to arrange themselves into any significance. She assumed they were boats, circling forever clockwise like a group of mechanical ice skaters, or precious stones swung on the end of a string, first toward Axehold, then slanting back toward town.

There were fewer boats now that summer was almost over, but more stars. They circled too tightly; it was hard to tell which were which. But as she watched, one hard point of light detached itself from the others and made right for them, as if someone had suddenly let go of the string.

"Here he comes."

Kathy came back to make sure. It was still a long way off. You couldn't hear the motor. They watched it for a while without saying anything.

"Can he be trusted?"

"Who?"

"Tangier."

"Oh, I don't know. I suppose so. Jack found him, not me. And God knows where. He finished off the Robertson's and they had no trouble collecting. I think Jason used him, too. So he comes highly recommended. . . . And besides, he hates us. He's crippled or something."

"I thought Jack said he needed the money."

"That too. Or he's black I think he said. What difference does it make? Maybe he's all those things. He's wretched and he'll do it cheap, just out of hate."

"And besides," she said, not bothering to lower her voice, "he can have the girl."

She seemed waiting for an argument. When Amy said nothing

she walked deliberately over to where the girl was sitting, stood there, then came back, smiling in a self-congratulatory way.

"Why not? She's pretty enough I suppose. What else can we do with her?"

Amy was usually ready to forgive Kathy anything, but tonight.... She was tired, she was worried about the twins, confused by the droning voice from the hammock. She couldn't help blaming Kathy for bringing all this down on them anyway. She had smuggled a radio in when they came out in August.... For when you go fishing and leave me here all alone she said when they discovered it . . . the first time any of them had broken the rule. Atlas was going to hurl the radio into the surf, such was his wrath as Jack put it, but by then they knew the end was near so they decided to save it for the weather forecasts.

"Jack was right, Kathy. Leave her alone."

"Then who is?"

"No one. I'm just saying...."

"We all are, Amy. We're all to blame, even that," and she pointed over her shoulder toward the sea. "So what? So insurance companies lose a few thousand now and then. So we'll buy a new place somewhere else.... And I know what you've been doing too, Al," she said, raising her voice. "He's been trying to make it easier for us. Right, Al? You're trying to make it easier for us, aren't you?"

Atlas' pace had slowed. He had gone from a steady heartbeat-like regularity to a slower, more intermittant speed and at times it seemed like he had stopped altogether. But then, just when it seemed as if he *had* stopped, they would hear the faintest breath of a word that just barely made it across the deck. Most of them they had never heard of now.

"It must be terrible in there," Kathy said. "It's hot enough out here with nothing on. How can he stand . . . I wonder how he can stand it."

And a few minutes later, when she opened the refrigerator door to check on whether they had left anything there, you could see from the light a dark narrow stain running the length of the hammock.

It was too dark. Kathy went into the bedroom for the lantern and put in on the edge of the deck.

"One if by land," she said. "The last match."

Amy laughed. It was quieter now, easier to ignore the occasional whisper of sound that seemed leaking through the weave of hammock behind them. And it was good to be alone again with Kathy. Whether it was the soft light from the lantern, or the dreamy way the surf ran in toward shore, they suddenly found themselves getting nostalgic.

"Well, why not," Amy said, when she sensed Kathy was beginning to laugh at her. "It's important to remember the good times."

Kathy shook her head.

"No. They're all out there, twenty-five feet ago. I think we should remember the bad times tonight. Bad times make it easier to leave."

"The time we ran aground on Jack's boat. Remember? Or when the twins found the poison ivy. You're right. I'll never forget...."

"Oh, Amy! Can't you do any better than that? I mean those are good times compared to.... You never listen, do you? Never mind. I'm sorry. We may as well play at something safe until he gets here."

"Play at what?" Jack asked, up from the beach. He was disappointed they had seen Tangier before he had.

"The bad times," Kathy said. "You should be good at that."

"Yeah, well...." He hesitated for a second. "How about 88 Walnut Lane, Arlington, New Jersey."

"Arlington, New Jersey?" Amy started to giggle.

"Yeah. 88 Walnut. Apartment 3B. ThreeB's right, isn't it, Kathy? Or had you forgotten?"

"Never mind, Amy. He thinks he's hurting me."

"Or Nuyens Park."

"Where's that?" Amy asked, not realizing how stupid it was until she saw the way the two of them were staring at each other.

"We all have our own," Kathy said, turning away. "Don't pay any attention to him."

"Or East 74th Street," he said, this time with a little laugh. "Especially East 74th Street."

Kathy got up and walked over to the lantern. The yellow cone of light caught her in her hard, sunburned stomach.

"It doesn't hurt anymore, Jack, so forget it. It just doesn't hurt anymore."

She covered the chimney with her hand and the light went out. In the quiet you could hear the boat now, the pitch of a large motor dampened in regular pauses through the waves. It was time to get ready but each of them seemed reluctant to move, mesmerized by the sound of the engine, the way it blended with the voice from the hammock.

"He hasn't had a thing since breakfast," Amy explained. She found a candle and put it by the food so he could see it when he got out.

"He's taking it hard."

When no one answered she went back to where she had been sitting and started groping around for her sneakers. In an hour, she thought, I'll be with the twins. In an hour I'll be with the twins.

She had the left sneaker and she thought she had found the right one, too, but then it moved and she realized it was Kathy's, that Kathy was doubled over by the railing, her body rocking back and forth in dry little sobs.

"The bastard!" she finally managed to whisper. "I'll never forgive him for reminding me. Never!"

Amy put her arm around her, but then her hand touched her breast and she drew it quickly back.

"I could mention a few places myself. I'll kill the bastard with them!" she whispered. "I'll kill him!"

"He's just kidding us, that's all," Amy said. "You know how they like to tease." But despite herself she moved away.

After that there was almost nothing. She would only remember Atlas' voice . . . hardly a whisper, hoarse, a grating sibilant sound like the hiss of surf wasting itself across the sand.

And for no reason at all Amy felt so relieved she couldn't keep it to herself any longer.

"No. You're all wrong. What we should talk about are the things we share. The wind, the stars. . . ." She hesitated for a moment, expecting Kathy to make fun of her. ". . . this beach."

Nothing. She opened the refrigerator for the light, then realized they were gone. But it was too much to keep inside herself. She felt so carefree, so light and happy . . . she had to share it with someone.

"There's so much in the world," she said, almost to herself. "There really is. There really is." And thinking about it made her ache.

She had to share it. Atlas was still asleep. She walked down the beach looking for Jack and Kathy. Somewhere along the way she took off her bathing suit, dropping it self-consciously onto the sand, then picking it up again before deciding to leave it there. It was good to be naked under the stars. When Atlas first brought her to Axehold ten years ago they had spent their first night together on the beach, her head against his chest as he recited the names of all the constellations that crossed the sky above them. She had fallen asleep to the sound . . . she thought she would give anything to have that moment again.

She walked all the way to the seawall without finding them. She was standing there about to call when—as suddenly as anything had ever happened—her mood vanished. She realized in horror that clouds were running in now with the surf, that her legs were wet, that she was alone on the beach. She started running toward the house, her feet slipping in the water, then saw the pile of furniture dissolve into a wave that was over her head, then a writhing paleness on a slight rise in the sand that stiffened and relaxed as the water separated around it and she realized it was Jack and Kathy, Kathy's feet kicking frantically against Jack's back in the same way the twins' had when Atlas carried them into the surf. And then just before the house a darker shape slipping in from the waves, moving quickly toward the pile at the bottom of the deck, a torch made of newspaper in either hand.

When they were alone again the girl stretched her legs and got up, going over to the rail on the far side of the sundeck. She raised herself on her toes, then reached down to touch them like a ballerina. Her blouse was already off; she turned her back to the hammock and pushed her shorts down over her legs, then stood there expectantly facing the sea, as if waiting for someone to come up from behind and put their arms around her. She acted surprised when no one did.

The voice from the hammock had never stopped.

"Warsaw. Vietnam. . . ."

The girl was shaking her head, smiling, running her hands down her legs, then back up over her arms. She went over to the hammock and got down on her knees, leaning her head down playfully against the floor near the candle.

"Stowe."

At first there was no reaction.

"Stowe."

There seemed to be the briefest kind of hesitation from the hammock.

"Hiroshima," the voice said again, but it seemed tentative now. The hammock had definitely swayed.

"Acapulco," she said, pretending not to notice, still stroking herself in the same self-confident way. "Big Sur."

"Lubyanka."

"Yellowstone."

"Dachau."

"Riviera."

"NagasakiDresdenGallipoli," but there seemed less and less conviction; she thought she could see his hand reach out from the hammock.

"Axehold," she coaxed. "Axehold, Axehold, Axehold."

The barest bit of flesh lifted itself free of the fabric.

"Axehold?"

"Axehold," the girl said, but for the first time there was doubt. "Axehold, Axehold," she said, starting to pout. "Axehold."

Then the entire arm. Then one leg. For a moment it seemed like he would get out and come to her. She backed up, trying to coax him even more, but she tripped over the glass Jack had left there and sprawled awkwardly back against the rail.

"Axehold," it said, and slipped back into the hammock for good.

"No," she said. "No, it's not like that. You're wrong!"

"Axehold," it said and that was all.

"No! You're wrong! No!"

And when Amy came back she found the girl there on her knees by the hammock, pounding at the lump with her fists and screaming at the top of her voice.

"Disneyland USA! Disneyland USA!"

"Bitch!"
Someone yelled from the beach.
"For God's sake hurry!"
She pulled her away, taking Atlas' head into her arms.
"It's all right," she whispered. "Everything's all right. . . . Shh! Everything's all right."
She finally felt him relax. With a shrugging motion his head fell onto her shoulders.
"Montpelier, Lansing, Albany," he said.
And because she held him so tightly she couldn't see how old he had become or the expression of contempt with which he looked over her head toward the sea she was able to tell the others when they came back that Atlas, strong Atlas, had left them in peace.

Erotifictions

ALVIN GREENBERG

1.

Many stories go to extravagant lengths to introduce an erotic scene, but not this one, which begins with the couple writhing on the living room floor, their clothing in spectacular disarray. There are enough lights blazing to illuminate the stage set for a pornographic movie: floor lamps, table lamps, spots on the paintings, a gauche plastic candelabra hung from the center of the ceiling. Because of an electrician's mistake, all the wall outlets are cued to the switch by the front door, so obviously this scene began when the couple entered the apartment, flicked on the wall switch—their coats, flung at the chair beside the doorway, landing instead on the floor—and, caught up in passion, couldn't take the time to switch off all these lighting fixtures one by one. Or perhaps it began even before that—at dinner (Chateaubriand, Grande Marnier), in the selection of clothes to wear for the evening, in a single glance during their first encounter many years ago... who can say where the roots of passion lie?

The passionate couple, however, prone on the living room floor, could hardly be said to lie, so fervent, so ceaseless, is their motion. The hands that peel back his shirt from his shoulders move with such speed and precision they could be either his or hers. The shoe that arcs away from them to drop into the silence of blue pile carpeting seems guided by no visible hand. They are both middle-aged, but her breasts as they burst suddenly from the cover of her black dress into the glare of all these lights could cause young movie stars to weep with envy, and his small ass flickering whitely over her bring both sexes to the high pitch of pure lust. All clothing shed now, mouths locked together, her legs vined around his, his hands stretching down behind her back to clutch her buttocks, their hips plunging faster and faster together gradually begin to slow, almost stop. A tiny sigh escapes—his—a quiet laugh—hers —and they roll soundlessly over. She rises, kneeling over him at first, then sitting on him, head tilted back so that her long hair falls behind her, breasts thrust far out, and then she begins to move once more. He lies still at first, his arms spread wide on either side, palms up, then, as her broad hips surge in a faster, heavier rhythm over his narrow ones, his head begins to roll soundlessly from side to side, his hands turn over, his fingers clutching at the thick carpeting, her mouth opens wide, a rising series of sighs enveloping his, him, his hips thrust at last upward, into motion, his back arched, his ass clear of the floor, a single, continuing moan—his, hers . . . who can say where the limits of passion lie?

In a few minutes, doubtless, they will begin again, their passion unlimited. As he flicks out the lights of the car in the restaurant parking lot, she will reach over and unzip his fly. As he sits up in bed in the morning, she will lean open-mouthed over his naked lap. As she stands at the sink pouring herself a glass of milk, he will move up behind her, raising her nightgown. As she lies in the rectangle of sunlight on her living room floor masturbating, he comes in from the kitchen and beings to shed his own clothes at once. As he enters her apartment, they begin again. His apartment. The car again. A motel on the outskirts of the city. A friend's cabin in the woods. The middle of the night. Early morning. Later in the morning. They began again. Again. If not them, then someone else. They begin again. Beginnings are so easy. It is easy, after all, to begin with the couple writhing on the living room floor, their clothing in spectacular disarray. But who can say where, if anywhere, the ends of such beginnings lie?

2.

On the thousand and second night Scheherazade prepared to climb into bed, ready for silence, resigned to sex, at last. As she let her siken robe slip from her bare shoulders, the array of oil lamps whose brilliance had for almost three years now outlasted both her glittering stories and the nights themselves, revealed a body as beautiful as it had been when she first came to the palace. But once she was beneath the linen sheets, the King, who had lain on the opposite side of the bed avidly watching her undress, made no move toward her. Side by side they lay on their backs in the great bed, naked beneath the sheets, a full two feet of unwrinkled linen between them, watching the reflection of the countless lamps shine in the gold-leaf ceiling high above them, turning the room bright as day.

Hours passed—the cries that marked their passing filtered softer than the desert breezes through the curtained windows—and still they lay there, neither sleeping nor moving. Their black hair spread damply against each of their delicately embroidered pillows and each of their bodies, beneath the sheets, lay encased in a fine sheath of sweat. Their moist eyes, turned steadfastly upward, reflected the lamplight almost as bright as did the ceiling when at last, not two hours before the dawn, the King broke their long silence.

"Scheherazade," he said softly, not even turning his eyes toward her, "after so great a time one no longer seems even to know how to begin. Perhaps you had better tell me a story again, just this one last time."

"My Lord," she replied, her own eyes carefully fixed upon the golden ceiling, "I do not know how to answer you. I have already told you all my stories. Perhaps I have even told you all the stories that there are. In order to tell you a story now, I would have to begin all over again. And I wonder if we really want to begin all over again, only to end up in exactly the same place, on another night precisely like this one, on opposite sides of this lonely bed, with hardly enough time left in the night to begin anything before the first birds are singing in the garden outside the bedroom and dawn brightens the curtained windows and the lamps start to sputter and smoke? And even if I were to begin again, would you not interrupt me at once to say, 'I remember that one, just as if it were yesterday that you told it to me'? Why, as soon as I began with 'Once upon a time....'"

"Yes, indeed," said the King, rising on his elbows and turning toward Scheherazade as he interrupted her, "I remember that one quite well, almost as if it were just yesterday that you told it to me. Please continue."

Now it was Scheherazade who sat up in bed, straight up, so that the sheet slid down off her breasts which, moist with a fine coating of sweat, glistened in the lamplight like freshly-washed fruit. "Once upon a time, then," she began again, "a beautiful young woman was brought to wed the King, who reclined in his bedchamber, robed in gold lamé, avidly watching...."

"Ah, *that* first story," reminisced the King, eyes ablaze. "Yes, I remember that, too. Exactly how I felt that night. Feel. 'Avidly watching,' indeed. It all begins to come back to me now. I begin...."

"And tomorrow night," said Scheherazade as it all began, birds singing, light through the curtains, spluttering, smoking oil lamps,

"I suppose I shall have to tell yet another story, one which begins 'On the thousand and third night....' "

3.

Her floor-length skirt, worn so low about the hips that it is decorated, beneath the round curve of her belly, by a fringe of brown, curly hair, is all she has on. She has a hawk-like nose and long, unbrushed hair, which hangs mostly down her back, partly forward, over her shoulders, along her breasts, which also hang low, nipples pointing outward, away from each other. She stands motionless on a small, square, wooden platform at the front of the room, and each time she is touched on the shoulder by the long wooden pointer she turns a few degrees to the right and then stands motionless again. After a great many such small turns, she finds herself precisely where she started, facing a chalkboard covered with symbols she cannot read, her back to the room while the lecturer, holding the pointer where she cannot see it, drones on and on in a language she cannot understand. After many minutes in this position, during which the pointer approaches her only once, to lift her hair from her back and let it fall again, the lecturer falls silent, and almost at the same instant a bell rings somewhere outside the room and she can hear the students, the audience—in the glare of the lights that shine on her when she is facing them she has no way to define them clearly—begin to gather up their things and leave the room, making strange liquid sounds as they go, not at all like any sounds she can recall herself from when she was a student.

She hears the door shut, a light switch click, feels the coolness spread over her back and shoulders as the spotlights go out, but does not move. Then suddenly the pointer slams viciously down across her buttocks, just below the beltline of her skirt, and she goes down quickly onto one knee beneath the pain. Again the pointer strikes, slicing its full violence across her right buttock now, and she slides down on both her knees, leans forward on her hands, her breasts drooping below her. Before she can prepare for the next blow, the pointer slides under her armpit, lifts her back up to a standing position, moves to her shoulder to turn her around to face the darkened room, then edges its way slowly down her body, its tip circling each breast, touching each nipple in turn, outlining her hips, gliding cross her belly and then dipping to unhook the simple loop of her belt. Her skirt drops around her feet. The pointer moves on downward, touching, drawing back, touching, drawing back. She does not look at it, cannot know, as it slides through her pubic hair, parts her lips, when, after drawing back, it will descend upon her again in violence. She dares not even turn her head to the side, can only stare straight outward, above the insidious caress of the pointer, into the room which, her eyes adjusting at last to the darkness, she sees is not wholly empty after all. One person has remained after the bell—or perhaps entered after the bell, while the others were departing from this scene, she has no way of knowing—seated now in the very center of the front row, alone, straining forward as if to read the next line the pointer will write vividly across her tensed body, much like the tender, unhealed lines it traces now on the soft skin of her inner thigh, lifts from, hesitates, descends to touch again, lifts, hesitates, touches, the lone spectator tensing visibly with each small hesitation, leaning forward with each potential slash, easing back as the descent become a caress, tensing as the pointer withdraws again, hesitates above the tender flesh . . . until suddenly the lecturer turns, thrusts the pointer into the spectator's tensed and ready hand, says—in English, so clearly the woman herself is startled by the clarity of her understanding—Here, you've involved yourself with this now, take the stick, do it, write the next line yourself. The way you want. The way you must. Do it. You.

4.

Alfred has a supernumerary pair of nipples: rather ridiculous, he thinks, when he has never been able to see any sense in even the one pair men normally have. The extra nipples are quite small, set about four inches below the normal pair, a little tuft of hair growing from each. No one ever noticed them—not Alfred himself or his parents or his friends on the swimming team or, later, even his wife, normally a very observant person when it came to anomalies—until a doctor remarked them during a routine physical examination. On the examination form lying on the doctor's desk was a diagram of the human figure, and Alfred, turning from front to back and side to side as the doctor commanded him and trying to hold himself as erect and healthy-looking as possible for a man with a habitual slump, was surprised to see the doctor make two small pencil marks on the figure's lower chest. The pencil still poised over the diagram as Alfred pulled his clothes back on, the doctor explained what the dots represented, supernumerary breasts, of no significance whatsoever. Then the pencil descended again and Alfred, tying his shoes, watched the doctor doodle all over the diagram of his body. Alfred did not like having his body doodled on.

Alfred *does* like breasts, though not his own, not even all four of them. Perhaps, he thinks after this anatomical discovery, this is what he gets for liking breasts so much: another pair of his own. He stands naked facing himself in the full-length mirror in his lover's bathroom, his skin glowing strangely in the light of the fluorescent plant-growing bulbs which she has substituted for the ordinary fluorescent lights in the fixtures on either side of the mirror. No one who doesn't already know they're there will ever notice them, he thinks. He turns sideways, gazing at his body in profile alongside a formica vanity top packed tightly with a dozen or more different varieties of African violets, assuring himself that nothing protrudes which should not protrude, that he is not a freak, not like these African violets, each differing from the others in color or shape of flower, leaf size or leaf design. Just as he is about to leave this humid, purple region of self-doubt, his lover enters the bathroom behind him, kicking off her shoes in the doorway, the fur collar of her coat still dusted with snow, cold against his back as she hugs him from behind, reaching her arms around him to pluck at his nipples with fingertips icy, vibrant.

"Don't do that!" he snaps, turning to face her.

"Alfred doesn't *like* his nipples caressed," she says softly, letting her hands, still cold, begin to descent toward other parts of his body. He had told her dozens of times that he doesn't feel anything when she caresses his nipples; *women* have sensitive nipples: what he likes is how her own stiffen and rise at his hands float above them, not even touching. Now her hands, fingers outspread, drift lightly, barely touching, down his body. She kneels on the oval rug in front of him, drops of melted snow in her collar giving off a glittering, violet fluorescence of their own. He feels her cool lips brush across his belly, her hands, just above, touch, move off, touch again, her forefingers probing as if at some new discovery though they have explored his entire body countless times before. At least she draws her head back, pauses, looks up at him.

"Alfred, what are these little bumps here? Do you feel anything?" she asks, probing at them with her forefingers again.

"No," he lies, though he can feel his whole body quiver as her fingers flick back and forth over his tiny extra nipples, knows his stiffening penis is already betraying him, "nothing, I don't feel anything there at all." All the same, he does not ask her to stop now as she lies back on the oval shag rug and, using one fingertip on each hand, draws him down on top of her.

5.

The sheer spectacle of the show takes Wanda's breath away. In the dim lighting, tiers of ornate, curving staircases rise gracefully from the stage: four staircases on the first level leading to a long platform, then three staircases rising to another platform, two staircases, yet another smaller platform, and then one final staircase spiralling out of sight. As the lights go up, Wanda sees that the staircases are lined with people, and her mouth opens in awe at the sheer number of them packed onto the staircases and platforms, women in long, low-cut white gowns and feathery headdresses, men in top hats and elegant, skin-tight black suits. Of course, thinks Wanda, dancers! And gradually the tableau before her gives way to motion. There must be music, but Wanda's eyes so dominate the whole experience that she hears nothing. The lighting changes: instead of a bright light spread evenly over the whole scene, broad-beamed spotlights sweep across the staircases now as the dancers begin to glide along them, a simple pattern at first of the women descending and the men ascending, such a smooth, unbroken flow that Wanda can barely discern their legs in motion, then a sudden reversal—sudden, though Wanda cannot define exactly when it took place—to the men descending and the women ascending, then a pattern of movement at once so simple and so elaborate that Wanda's hands clench with excitement. The men and the women continue to move up and down the staircases, across the intervening platforms, each in their separate lines, their motion as smooth and graceful as that of the spotlight beams sweeping across them, but now they flow in intricate pathways, up some of the staircases and down others, across platforms, the lines of men and women sometimes gliding precisely in step with each other, sometimes flowing counter to each other, even at times, where the stairways and platforms intersect, flowing *through* each other. Wanda wants to jump up and down in her seat with excitement—never in her life has she seen such a spectacular array of grace and complexity!—but she knows she dare not and controls herself by plunging her clenched fists tightly together in her lap.

Now, as Wanda watches amazed, the dancers are all flowing downward together, off the stair, off the platforms. For a moment the lights stop moving and there is a great waterfall of dancers, their costumes glittering black and white as they cascade downward to the stage level. Then it seems as if the whole stage is being tilted forward toward Wanda. Her chest begins to tingle and she clamps her fists tightly together between her thighs. The lights are moving again and the dancers too, but now she sees them from above, the white feathery headdresses, the black top hats, the dancers spinning slowly clockwise, the lights turning counterclockwise against them, making the dancers, she realizes, seem to be moving much faster than they really are. But now she realizes that they are moving faster, faster and faster, that their motion, their design, shifts and shifts again, almost too rapidly for her to keep up with. At one moment she sees long alternating lines of black and white radiating outward from the center of their circle, swaying like some many-tentacled octopus as they spin, and then abruptly concentric circles of black and white, turning clockwise and counterclockwise against each other, and then with equal suddenness a single spiralling line of alternating black and white spinning like films she has seen of the great nebula around a center brightly lit by a single spot. Wanda rocks back and forth in her seat, hands squeezed tensely between her thighs, as the whirling spiral squeezes in upon its bright center, opens out, squeezes tight again, opens, squeezes, opens, squeezes . . . until without warning the center goes suddenly dark and Wanda releases a great sigh, aware at the same time—she realizes it is the first thing she has actually *heard* all this while—that a sigh has risen from the audience all around her as the stage falls darks and the house lights begin to come up and she leans back, panting, glancing at her parents seated on either side of her, both of them openmouthed, breathing heavily, and no one, in the whole theater, standing, yet, to leave.

6.

The beautiful cows stand in the green pasture, their breath steaming in the chilly early morning air. The blond boy picks through the garbage cans in the alley behind the all-night diner. The old poet sits at his typewriter, one hand out of sight, buried up to the wrist in his open fly. The well-mannered dog strains heavily against the chain that fastens him to his doghouse; his nose binds him to everything that happens in the neighborhood. The teen-aged girl tosses sweatily in her sleep, shredding the pages of the fashion magazine trapped in the tangled bedding with her. The telephone lineman, up all night working on the damage from last weekend's storm, sits in his truck, watching the bubbles that froth up in his plastic cup as he pours the luke-warm coffee from his thermos. The left-fielder sits on the floor of the motel room, his back against the wall, kneading the cramps from his calves. The young mother runs hot water into the tub; it is the only time of day she can soak in the bath without interruption. The gelding that has chewed through its tether moves through suburban backyards. The adolescent returns from delivering the morning papers and locks himself in the bathroom. The dark-haired lady in her fifties sits in the living room chair she has not moved from since she returned from the concert at midnight, her eyes still open and her fur coat still closed about her. The calico cat slinks from one side of the cool fireplace hearth to the other. The young rabbi dreams of water, endless vistas of water. The muskrat plunges into the algae-covered pond. The red-winged blackbirds settle on the swaying cattails. The third-grade teacher whose chenille bathrobe has lost all its buttons eats her breakfast cereal with the silver sugar spoon while she watches the morning news on television. The letter carrier's headache is so severe he makes mistake after mistake sorting the mail for his morning rounds. The dead guinea pig's body is hidden in sawdust in the corner of the cage. The four-year-old rides her rocking horse through the curtained darkness of her bedroom. The sleeping men locked in each other's arms, the secretary lying awake anticipating the sudden buzz of her alarm clock, the zoo keeper forking a dripping chunk of horsemeat through the bars of the panther's cage, the interns drowsing in their seats in the operating room amphitheater, the woman who drives the yellow school bus around the shores of the lake, the children who rise and dress to ride the yellow school bus, the dreamer of water, the fish, the multitudinous dreamers of water....

It is morning. The day is just beginning, the light just now rising on its possibilities, and each of these sentences, like every other sentence you have ever read, is the beginning of a curious, tense, provocative, charming, brutal, elusive, disgusting, amusing, stimulating, shocking, ordinary—and erotic—fiction.

Prayer

STUART DYBEK

He spiralled away from the party hugging the banister up the smokey perspective of stairs that threatened to extend infinitely, climbing slightly off-balance like ascending an unplugged escalator.

The bathroom was at the top. It didn't seem to have a door. He could still hear the Indian music from down below. The mirror on the medicine cabinet reflected the eerie gleams of a candle burning inside the toilet bowl.

So he ended up micturating out the bathroom window. To accomplish this he had to kneel on the floor squeezed in between the curving lip of the bathtub and the windowsill. The window had bars on the outside which he carefully stuck his penis through. He felt the wind along the building streaming his urine away, some of the drops spraying back in on him. He wondered if anyone was below, feeling for raindrops with their open palms.

He turned partially around in order to gauge how to best extricate himself. That's when he first realized she was there watching, the flickering candle throwing streaks across her knees, her face still in shadow.

His startled impulse was to jerk around back to facing the window without acknowledging her. He still hadn't zipped himself back up having intended to wait till he was standing. Now he was too paralyzed with embarrassment to reach down and fumble with his crotch, so he folded his hands and bowed his head against them in the posture of deep prayer.

"I'm sorry if I disturbed you," she said.

"It's all right," he said without looking up, "I should have chosen another room." The draft from the open window made him uncomfortably aware of his still exposed member.

"Will you be much longer," she asked, "I have to use the bathroom."

"I'm almost finished," he said. "I'm praying for my mother. She died of cancer last week. I made a promise to her on her deathbed that I'd pray for her once each day. I remembered just at midnight that I hadn't prayed today."

"It's about one in the morning *now*."

"I know, I thought as long as I was up here praying while one day was ending and another beginning I might as well get both at once."

"Well, if you don't mind I'll just *go*. Just keep praying, don't turn around, okay? With these coulottes you have to get all undressed."

"Okay," he said. He heard her bones crack, probably her shoulders as her arms went up to undo the zipper. He was getting an erection and adjusted his posture so it could pass through the bars. Five stories below was anyone looking up?

"There's a goddamned candle in the toilet," she said.

"I noticed when I first came in."

"If that's the way they are I guess I'll just have to go in the sink. A person's only human. It's only number one . . . I'll run the water," she added somewhat apologetically.

He heard the sink creaking as she boosted herself onto it and envisioned her straddling it naked in his mind's stoned eye. An image he half erased by thinking that if this were Europe everything would seem natural. But his body was unconsciously swaying back and forth, his erection rubbing gently between the rusty bars.

"Tee-hee," she giggled tipsily, "the porcelain's cold."

A sympathetic chill shot up the back of his thighs peppering his prostate gland with goosepimples. He heard the water running into the sink and then the sound mingled with a liquid hiss.

"Oh God!" she sighed, "I've been holding that all night. I should never drink coffee on top of beer. It never sobers me up anyway. I think maybe I've got weak kidneys or something. Like you know on those psychological tests when they ask you: 'Do you feel like you urinate more often than others?' I took one that asked that one time when I was thinking of quitting Woolworth's and going into the Peace Corps. I didn't though—join the Peace Corps, that is. Maybe I do feel like I urinate more often than others. But I marked no on the test. It's obvious what they're looking for. You put down yes and they think you're some kinda nut. Like paranoid, you know? But what if you really do? See, what they're really getting if somebody does, but won't admit it, is someone smart enough to see through their tricks, but not somebody honest, you know what I mean?"

He was pumping himself hard between the bars. His head banged into the window sash just as he felt a cramp coming on in one of his legs, and toppling backwards to unbend the leg his spine smacked against the lip of the bathtub.

"Hey!" She jumped off the sink, "you alright? You having some kind of mystical experience or something?"

He was lying flat on his back on the cool terrazzo floor. She was bending over him, her breasts swaying just above, their tips administering little slaps in the face like bringing him around.

Slowly, like a man arising from the dead, he raised his face into the face-shaped space between her breasts, twisting his head from side to side grinding smooches from one nipple to the other.

"Oh, oh, why am I letting you do this," she was saying. Her head was tilted back as if she was addressing the ceiling.

When he slid into her he could feel the fleshy smoothness coat the grooves the rusty bars had chaped into his erection.

"Oh wow! Zowie! am I drunk! am I high!" he heard her repeating as their bodies stretched and snapped back together till his every thrust was rewarded with a bullseye and her breath his breath somebody's breath falling about his ears echoing back off the tile like splashing water.

The first thing he heard after he came was the drip from the faucet striking the still surface of lukewarm water in the bathtub. Each plip sent rings of small ripples breaking against his throat. He wondered how they'd ended up in the bathtub.

His legs angled out like a frog's from where his ankles were tangled together in his trousers. She lay quietly between them. He could hear the faucet still running in the sink across the way, gurgling down the drain, the water trickling around the elbow joint. The Indian music was still floating faintly up the stairs, the sounds of the party seemed to climb towards them, people blowing paper horns unrolling with feathers at their ends, cranking noisemakers. The bathroom began to fill with revelers holding votive candles in their fingertips. They gathered silently around the bathtub, holding their candles aloft, the curved sides of the tub and water reflecting the orange flickers.

"Was that true?" she whispered.

"What?"

"About your mother dying of cancer last week?"

They set their candles carefully into the water. A few drops of hot tallow sizzled. The candles bobbed and floated around them, their tiny flames catching the drafts like sails. Just his slightest movement could capsize them all.

The Love of Beasts

JERRY BUMPUS

Sunday evening. The woman in black, the thin young woman in the second pew, is the minister's wife, Maureen. Look! She leans forward as if she will kneel between the pews, though William hasn't yet called for that; later, at the climax of his sermon, he will rear back and command the congregation to humble themselves on the floor of God's house.

Maureen's eyes appear closed tight. Perhaps she is searching for a vision of William and God locked in a holy grapple that will consecrate him, Maureen, and the entire congregation. But let us move nearer.

Her lips are thin and bloodless purple, the lips of an ascetic. Her eyes are open a tiny crack through which she sees an empty gray field. Maureen can rise and walk off into that field....

Suddenly the church is quiet. But Maureen doesn't lift her head; William often pauses, letting the congregation appal itself with silence.

A deacon on the front row turns, for William is staring toward the back of the church. Maureen turns, and she is the first to speak, if it can be called that: to the congregation's great amazement and shame, Maureen fills the church with a loud wet sucking sound.

"Praise God," William says again and again. Women are sobbing. The deacon takes another turn embracing Andrew.

"I'm sorry," Andrew says loudly.

"I am thankful," William says for everyone to hear. "All of us are thankful. At last my brother has returned. Praise God!"

"I should have stayed outside," Andrew says. "Till you got it done."

William raises his voice: "This is God's work."

"Praise God," they murmur.

"Let us kneel," William says. "Let us put our knees on the floor of God's house humbly and offer thanks for the return of this prodigal person." His voice rises—"The prodigal has returned. From evil, the prodigal has returned. From black sin where he walked, the prodigal has returned...."

Maureen has knelt but she does not bow her head. She watches Andrew, her eyes wide. He is grinning at her.

The deacon and a handful of others come to the parsonage and sit at the kitchen table drinking coffee while William discusses Andrew's career of sin.

Standing by the stove, Maureen watches Andrew. He wears a green suit several sizes too small, a white shirt, and a blue flowered tie. As William talks, Andrew nods his enormous head, and once he tries to add to William's remarks, but he stammers and stops. He sits holding the edge of the table with both hands, as if he might at any moment push it away or turn it over. His hands are huge. Maureen has never seen such fingers.

His face . . . Maureen is certain that in prison the guards put his head in a machine that squeezed it until it was twice as long as a normal head. His nose is huge, his eyes as big as eggs.

William finishes with Andrew's soul and leans back and yawns.

The deacon rises, reaches across the table and again shakes Andrew's hand. The others take a final turn, say good-night, and leave by the back door.

William and Andrew go into the living room, and Maureen washes the dishes. She smiles at her reflection in the black window over the sink. She stretches her mouth until the smile is a gash, her thin face arrogant, fierce. She balloons her cheeks, then gapes, showing all her teeth, her lips stretched until they hurt. She lolls her tongue and tilts her head, her tongue sliding from one corner of her mouth to the other. Sticking out her tongue as far as it will go, she closes her eyes and slowly licks her lips, around and around....

In the living room William says, "God forgives you, Andrew, and so do I, but we haven't forgotten, and we don't want you to ever forget what you did. You've had twelve years to repent for the life you stole from an innocent, unsuspecting person. I hope you prayed constantly those twelve years and looked deep into your heart. Did you?"

Andrew nods his big head.

"Good." The house is silent. William calls to the kitchen—"if you're done with those dishes, come in here."

Maureen enters and Andrew speaks to her: "She looks like the picture."

"What picture?" William says quickly.

Andrew's huge fingers carefully take a snapshot from his billfold. William glances at it—"Huh"—and hands it back.

"It was when you got married," Andrew says.

"Much has happened since then," William says. "To you, nothing has changed since you've been away. Because you're a fool, Andrew, you erroneously believe everything has waited. But *nothing* waited. You have been left behind. And now you come and lay at my feet the responsibility of your life."

Andrew lowers his head.

"To bed." William stands. "There's a cot in the basement. You can sleep there." William takes hold Andrew's elbow and steers him through the kitchen to the basement door. "Goodnight, Andrew. Tomorrow you begin a new life."

Maureen follows William upstairs. In her room as she undresses she feels Andrew listening. She knows he hears her open and shut her closet door and hears the creak of her bedsprings.

In Andrew's new life he follows at William's heels like a giant dog. People stare as they walk down the street, and William knows they are laughing. It occurs to him that for some reason

God has sent Andrew to punish him, and this sends William into a deep preoccupation. He continues with all his duties; but he is profoundly distracted. He revives now and then, such as the morning when William is "on the air" broadcasting the WIIOD "Holy Hour": he looks up and is alive—free!—for a bright, splendid moment. But then through the big studio window he sees Andrew sitting in the waiting room, his giant hands on his knees.

During the Wednesday night sermon William can barely see the congregation. The light in the church is strangely dim; before him the congregation seems submerged in a yellow pond.

Several days later when Andrew comes up from the basement William is waiting in the kitchen. Maureen is at the stove.

"Andrew, you can't come with me today," William says. "Or tomorrow. Not any more." Then William turns away. He cannot look at Andrew or at Maureen, who has turned. He avoids their eyes as if he were speaking to a Sunday school class of high school boys and girls. He looks at the floor, then the ceiling. "Andrew, the best thing for you is steady employment. I will find something for you."

Andrew stares down at his feet.

"Today," William goes on, "I will keep you in mind as I make my rounds. Jobs are scarce, but with my influence I will find...."

Andrew opens his mouth and makes a thick, low gargle which becomes words: "Inside I helped the chaplain. I was his 'sistant."

William nods. "Very commendable."

"I can be your 'sistant. I can do things."

William purses his kips. "Um," he says to the refrigerator. He rubs his eyes with the tips of his fingers. "All right. For the time being. Today you can sweep out the church and empty the ... empty the...."

"Waste cans," Maureen says.

"Yes." William gestures vaguely, as if he were brushing mosquitoes from his face. Then he turns to Maureen. "Isn't breakfast ready yet?"

Maureen cleans her bare little room and goes downstairs with her dirty bedsheets. As she passes the door to the living room, where Andrew is watching television, she doesn't look in. In the basement she puts the sheets in the washer and switches it on. In the noise under the low ceiling she can't hear him now if he walks from the living room. . . .

She goes to his cot. She closes her eyes, leans over it, and takes a deep breath. She yanks up the sheets and stuffs them into the washing machine with the others. She leans against the churning machine.

Upstairs she stands in the kitchen waiting, then she goes to the living room. Andrew sits in William's chair, his hands hanging over the ends of the arm rests. "Do you want a cup of coffee?" Maureen says.

"Sure." He rises from the chair and walks across the room, shaking the floor and the walls, making the tiny china dogs and cats skitter on their knick-knack shelves. Maureen turns off the television set. When she enters the kitchen he is sitting at the table and as she puts the coffee pot on the stove she feels him watching her.

He laughs loudly. "I used to think about this all the time." He shakes his big head. "Just this way. You and me would drink a cup of coffee. And here it is." His large eyes are unblinking. "I used to think about you all the time. I dreamed about you. Now here it is."

Maureen is sinking. Her eyes swallow everything into her. She turns to the stove.

She pours the coffee and sits across the table from him. He noisily drinks his coffee, puts down his cup, and grins. Then he rises and goes into the living room. He switches on the television set, and Maureen hears a boom of voices.

William comes home late that afternoon. He doesn't say hello but squints at Maureen, then goes through the kitchen and looks into the living room. Andrew sits before the television set. "Hello, William," he says.

William goes upstairs and stays in his room until Maureen calls him to supper. He eats fast, has face low over his plate, his bald spot staring at Maureen and Andrew. Maureen picks at her food. Then she feels William looking at her. She faces him, and his eyes shift down to his plate.

And Maureen almost cries out, for suddenly she knows that William wants it too.

Knowing takes her breath. Her face burns and she bows her head, unable to look at either of them, burning with shame and glee.

The next morning after breakfast William leaves in the car, and a few minutes later Andrew also leaves the house. Maureen watches him plod down the sidewalk toward town, swinging his arms. She stands at the window until he returns, carrying a paper sack. He goes straight downstairs.

That night William goes to the church for a board meeting and he allows Andrew to come along. Maureen goes to the basement.

Beside the cot is the paper sack, the top folded in a neat cuff, and in it are candy wrappers and cigarette butts which Andrew drowned out either under the faucet or with spit: she pictures him carefully drooling on a large finger and touching it to a cigarette.

A green transistor radio is smudged with chocolate fingerprints: she sees him holding it while he lies on his back....

Under the thin mattress are comic books, a pair of little scissors, and men and women and animals Andrew has cut out. There are also magazines of naked women smiling cruelly. She picks up another magazine, looks at it, and draws her elbows tight to her sides. The magazine is full of naked men standing

THE LOVE OF BEASTS

with their hands on their hips. The magazine slips from her fingers. She lies down on the cot and stares at the cobwebbed floorbeams overhead, her heart pounding hard. She tries to keep from thinking, but in spite of herself she sees the men in the magazine, one of them in particular: a handsome young man wearing a big sombrero grins and aims himself at Maureen.

*

The days are ponderous with hours, nights are endless as Maureen lies in bed lost to darkness, teeth clenched, eyes wide, afraid of what awaits her in sleep. She glides through the night with her legs apart.

Cooking their breakfast she leans against the stove without seeing the food or smelling it. William watches her constantly. Andrew eats enough for four men, then plods back down the basement stairs like a horse returning to its stable.

William's sermons are thrilling, inspiring, incoherent: words spurt out of control and ababble with damnation, he sees for them all a universe of sin, he analyzes the holy principle of wrath in goodness, and at the top of his lungs he speculates about devastating redemption.

Head bowed, Maureen listens to William, and squinting, she creates a swamp and places William in it wearing his black suit, his face perfectly round, his bald spot shining. In the swamp William preaches to stumps. The sky is a thick intersticing of snake scales.

On the afternnon of that inevitable day, William comes in the back door, and stops short as if he has been hit. His nostrils quiver. Sweat pops out all over his face. He *knows!*

At the stove Maureen doesn't turn to greet him. *That* speaks it!

And he can smell it in the house, like wet dogs.

"Is he here?" William says, his voice level though he is turning purple.

Leaning over the stove, Maureen shakes her head.
"Where? At town?"
"I don't know."
"All right," William says. He is panting. "All right. Then I will wait. Yes." He walks across the kitchen and back. "We will eat supper without him. Yes." His hands fly up and he claws his bald spot. "Immediately!" he shouts.

Maureen rushes back and forth between the table and the stove. William sits down and rattles off grace, not lowering his head but watching Maureen set the table. She walks stiffly. Her lips are pink and swollen.

She sits down and he can tell that at first it is painful for her to take food into her mouth. But then she eats faster and faster, greedily, chewing with her mouth open, stuffing food in with both hands, and she looks up at William, her nostrils flared, her eyes bright.... "Stop that!" he shouts.

In the silence they hear laughter below. "Agh," William says. His eyes bulge. He leaps to his feet and bounds across the kitchen and down the basement stairs. "Ah hah!" he yells and Maureen hears scuffling. William roars, then words emerge: "...again...damnation...obey. Listen to me. Damnation."

Splat! Someone is struck. Again—again. Maureen goes to the door and slowly walks down the stairs.

Andrew sits on his cot with his hands folded in his lap. His head jerks to the side when William strikes him.

William turns to Maureen, his fist drawn back. "There," he yells and points to a glint on the floor—a hunting knife. "Look what I found him playing with. And there. A gun."

Maureen can't see it . . . unless the spider shadow by the wall is a gun. Yes. Black and shrewd: a pistol.

"And these." William grabs a handful of magazines and throws them up. One is snagged by a nail in the floorbeams and hangs there. William knocks it fluttering across the basement.

"He will not change," William pants. "Twelve years. Murder. A man's *life*. For nothing. And the damnation. The eternal damnation!" William reaches down for the hunting knife....

Maureen backs toward the stairs. But William is only gathering up the knife and the gun. Holding them in one hand, he bends and picks up the magazine with the other.

William faces Maureen. "And you. *You*." His lips work, his face strains, but no words come. He goes upstairs.

Andrew pulls the sheet off his cot and crosses the basement to the faucet. He wets the sheet and holds it to his face. He returns to the cot and grins at Maureen. His face is swollen as if mushrooms bulge under the skin.

He goes down on his knees and reaches into the crack between two big cardboard boxes. He withdraws his hand and it holds what Maureen thinks at first are black bones. Andrew stands and puts his hand into the thing.

At the top is a hatchet; the other end of the short handle is a dagger. Set in the knuckle-guard are steel burrs. Andrew grins and chops air.

Maureen lies in the night waiting for sleep and death, but she knows she will never sleep again. But when the door opens she has been asleep, or in that dawn-quiet state between waking and the pandemonium of dreams. The shadow in the door isn't Andrew but William. He hesitates, his head turns back and forth—the room is unfamiliar—and he shuts the door behind him. The room is dark but she sees him, a shadow, moving toward the bed. "What do you want?" she says distinctly but not loudly.

He stops. "I. . . . ." She hears him opening and shutting his mouth. "You're my wife and. . . ."

"I don't care. I don't want you in here," she says louder. "This is my room."

She feels the nudge as he bumps the bed—she has guided him with her voice—and she moves toward the wall.

He talks louder, speaking swiftly and to Maureen's amazement in the dark William sounds like a young man. But his *words* reach her. She tries to ignore what he is saying, but with the determination of insects the words penetrate the dark.

She listens coldly. His voice now strangely boyish, William informs her they have been man and wife four years but there has never been love in their marriage. He had hoped she would find in herself the humility and holy resignation of love; but that not until this miraculous transformation, which William explains is true love, could they truly be married, and now she has demonstrated that she will never be capable only of base love, arrogant, prideful, the love of beasts.

So Maureen must go away. William will tell the church board that he woke one morning and she had vanished.

"Above all, I cannot abide what you have done to my brother," William says, still louder. "You will leave and I will guide him. If there can ever be hope in his pitiful existence, it can only come through my love. Tomorrow when you are gone he will come up to this room and sleep in this bed.

"Do you see how thoroughly you are rejected? Do you now see that you are evil and that I am casting you out? I could spend my entire life laboring for your salvation, but all my efforts would be for nothing. And meanwhile Andrew would sink into deeper ruination, for I cannot reach him with you in this house. You are a barrier between Andrew and me, and because he is simple and weak, you are stealing him away. I see it clearly.

"God has spoken to me, and His Word is clear. Though it means your ruin and the loss of your immortal soul, I must *cast* you out. Now all I can do for you, Maureen, is pray that someday you will open your heart and accept God's mercy on you and let Him *raise* you from your evilness. Oh, let us pray."

Maureen moves across the bed to kneel on the floor beside him. She reaches the edge and putting her feet down, discovers she has put her legs against William. Her gown has ridden up her thighs, and as Andrew glides into the room he sees William's head between Maureen's knees.

Maureen sits before the television set. The picture is on, the sound is off. Habits twit at the back of her mind: she could make coffee or clean the house, yes, she must clean the house, the mop and a bucket of water, first upstairs in her room, then the hall, the stairs, through the kitchen, the basement stairs....

The night is silent. Trembling, she stares at the television screen.

Andrew comes into the room. He has slicked down his hair and wears his green suit, shirt, and blue flowered tie. He walks across the room and picks up the telephone. "I want to go to St. Louis," he says into the receiver. "St. Louis," he says louder. "I don't have a number any more." He listens. "He is Robber Robber." Andrew turns to Maureen and says loudly, "Tell her." Maureen stares straight ahead. "His name," Andrew says. "*His* name. Robert . . ." into the phone—"*Robert*." He waits, listening. "Robert two times. Robber Robber."

Maureen watches the television screen. The night won't end. All the lights in the house burn but the room is dim and there are no windows or doors in the house and the house is filled with the smell of meat.

"Here." Andrew pulls her from the chair and across the room.

"What's he done this time?"—a man's voice in the phone.

"William?" Maureen says.

"Who is this?" the voice says. "Where's Andy?"

Maureen looks at Andrew's swollen face. His eyes are huge. He is nodding at her.

Maureen tells the voice in the phone the name of the town and the address of the parsonage.

It is day when Maureen opens her eyes. A man is talking to Andrew. He is as tall as Andrew and wears a gray sweater and a hood pulled over his head and drawn tight with a string, squeezing his face into a fist. "Okay. Her too." He looks at Maureen. "What's wrong with her?"

They lift her from the chair. "Christ," the man says. The seat of the chair is soaked.

Andrew brings clothes into the room and they dress her. Then they take her outside and put her in the back seat of a car. She wakes in a hotel room where brown men balloon from stains on the walls and ceiling. Andrew stands by the window cutting pictures from comic books.

Three cabins squat at the end of the dirt road. A wooden sign nailed to a fence post says Lake Vu. A mud-splattered car with its hood raised is parked in front of the center cabin, and an incredibly thin man, made of sticks, is working on the car. "There's Mr. Goforth," Robert says. The man walks over to their car and looks into the back seat at Maureen. His face is a gray, sharp triangle. "Well, well," Mr. Goforth says and laughs quickly.

They get out and go with him into the center cabin. There is a bed, a chair, and a sink with the faucets broken off.

Robert hands him some money and Mr. Goforth counts it. "Nice friends you got," Mr. Goforth tells Andrew. Andrew is wearing his suit and shirt and tie. His shirt is sweat-soaked and his suit is speckled with foodstains. Andrew stares at Mr. Goforth.

"You watch out for them, okay?" Robert says.

"Sure," Mr. Goforth says. "I'll come and watch. Ain't that right?" he asks Andrew. "That's real good citement."

Robert leaves and Mr. Goforth goes back out and works on his car. Andrew sits in the chair and starts cutting out a comic book. Maureen lies on the bed and mosquitoes hang in the air above her.

The hood of the car slams and Mr. Goforth comes into the cabin with a short three-legged stool. He picks up one of Andrew's cut-outs, a little man with a gun in his hand, and turning to Maureen, Mr. Goforth solemnly dances the little man in the air.

He sits on his stool and looks first at Andrew, then at Maureen. "You know what, Andy?" Andrew is busy. "I like a pretty face."

His smile is a crooked line in his face. "Is she real good to you, Andy?"

The cabin is silent.

Looking over his shoulder at Andrew, Mr. Goforth rises from the stool and moves to the side of the bed. "I love you," he whispers. His hand hovers over her face. A mosquito lands on the thumb. "Andy, I want to touch her."

He touches her cheek. She closes her eyes and he touches her eyelids. "You are beautiful," he whispers. He touches her lips and works a finger into her mouth. Leaning over the bed, he runs his hand up between her legs. He stops when she moans.

He goes out to his car and comes back with two pistols. "Here." Andrew holds them and grins.

Mr. Goforth speaks loudly: "When they get here, you tell them you got a message from Lead City, huh? Give me them things." Mr. Goforth goes to the door, cocks the pistols' hammers, and fires them. The gunfire shakes the cabin. In the ringing silence that follows Mr. Goforth hands the guns to Andrew. "They'll think you're a cowboy."

Mr. Goforth goes out the door and Maureen hears the car's starter grinding. Then the car starts and Mr. Goforth races the motor and it backfires. Andrew stands in the doorway, laughing and waving the pistols.

Mr. Goforth drives off and the sound of the motor hangs in the air as the car goes down the road.

Andrew walks around the room pointing the pistols, dodging, bending his knees, shaking the guns—*"Daah! Daah!"*—at the empty doorway. Then they hear the car.

Andrew steps out the door as the car comes nearer, and Maureen knows it is going to happen now, the car louder . . . It stops. A door slams. Then she hears Mr. Goforth.

He and Andrew come into the cabin. "Come on," Mr. Goforth tells her, and Maureen feels herself moving off the bed but she can't walk. He takes her arm and they walk outside. She squints in the sunlight.

Andrew is standing by the car, the guns in his hands, his long face watching Maureen and Mr. Goforth. "She is supposed to go with me," Mr. Goforth says. Andrew's mouth opens, but the sound is not words but a broken sigh, like a man humming in his sleep. "Just ask Robert Robert," Mr. Goforth says and opens the car door. He shoves Maureen in and slams the door. He goes around, gets in the other side, and starts the motor. He races the motor and they take off.

Maureen sees the trees on both sides of the road, and beyond the trees, empty fields. Faster, the trees blur by as the car bounces down the dirt road, and they top a hill and start down the other side. "Made it!" Mr. Goforth yells. "Hot damn!" He pounds the steering wheel. "What *do* you think of that?"

"Fine," Maureen says, hearing her voice and knowing for a moment that she is still inside this flesh, seeing large green trees, a sky.

My Trip to Southern California
On a Nine by Twelve Demo

PETER BLIND

One seat behind the engine in a vintage car, and littered fences by the railroad pool hall, the deserted St. James Hotel, John's flat walk house to Santa Cruz where Merrill got the dope by the knees and we all got sick on empty stomachs—married by Agnes O'Brien Smith cloistered in a concrete redoubt.

Wondering. About anything in an airport lobby with a man scrubbing the floor by hand, jobs are scarce. Nervous revellers laughing idly. A couple of military men in crisp fatigues as makeout artists seducing a pair of legs on a non-stop flight. The commissionaire arrives with handsome aide bound for distant meetings. Economy class has been sold out at the Continental counter, worried customer bargaining about the price hard as nails. Crouching in a corner waiting for a window to open, and "window" has a double you at both ends. It's a sad-ass situation, I don't want any part of it: endless cliche and poorly done at that going through changes for the big weenee. Legs, man, everybody in Ceremonial Modern Aire dress. Keep lust at bay. It's no use but it feels good and comforting. (Healthy legs, for Christ's sake, metallic ice cubes, too.) An hour to go but what a thrill! Through the door to authorized personnel country Santa Cruz Smokey calls and suddenly rushing so as to burst a gut to get upstairs and have a beer. I've got her in the

Meadows again. (The F.B.I. is watching me. The bartender is too. . . .) "Justify the price of your beer by drinking only the best." Jesus, it's *dead*. Dragging by on the waitress' feet. That fucking F.B.I. gut is putting my life into a capsule, shit, with flourishes & ruffles. All aboard killed, missing survivors linked to the S.L.A. running roughshod over plump matrons, ascending a neverending dictum at the prescribed angle and at the prescribed speed. Still at the bar with three drink tabs numbered 1735, 1752, and, within the bosom of Liberty, 1762. A long time ago the plucky bird chased the hawk.

Lined up now and the man says to the glass door, "You are relieved," just a minute before eating the roach brighteyed and bushytailed captured inside the beatle-black chair carrousel stuffed in. Innocence wants to see around the wing, but now on the plane *over* the wing. The ultimate captive audience with a grim crew, shit, smiling bravely on. Baggage boarded revving up Mr. Pratt & Mr. Whitney down to purple moire sunlight on silverized wings umbilical disconnected moving from left to right over the apron so slowly as the man in the middle wrings his hands: drinks are a dollar down from a buck fifty. And waiting a lifetime for it, less than half a pint of Old Number 7 above the clouds fighting turbulence, joystick tucked in the seat of our pants amid three dimensions explicitly done with a few heads popping up. The Time has come, we must get on with It, bourbon rocks loudly over the roar climbing about to descend into SoCal before the ice melts. Wanting that, too, in the middle of the night. . . .

The winds of the Santa Ana cool & strong, a flight of many swallows amid waving plants: touchdown to bar-bee-que beef jet fuel exhausted at an overcrowded void within eyeshot of the Birtcher Building. No ordinary lumberyard, this is a Home Improvement Center without bicycles or pedestrians. A helicopter gave me a lift to a door anxious to share impressions. Dry hockey games with mask and you get the gear and when you tend the precious goal, the slap dash scene with kids at Localiquor.

Still walking with the sun in the fields of wild, voluntary oats, railroad tracks lined with miles of green oats, then after no Mom & Pops in the heart of stoplights and imaginary intentions topped with allusions, I'm here quick making new friends skiing. The sky is cloudy shadowing a monumental two people; just rushing in too quick but being Brothers & Sisters, which makes you honest. Cory doesn't like the Cookie Monster so the trap is destroyed, layed to waste and my mind at a standstill looking for solutions: I want you to go away. Luke warm is O.K., I pray to God, so the sign says. A lowdown, stinking, greasy, chitlin-eatin' woman; get your big legs off me, Rebecca!

As Robbie slides in to whisk us off, we don't even need to stick to the *Truth!* (Something stuck in a molar.) **Will you** *light the fucker up?!* **And do not beauxgard so the catacombs wander in,** Lake Gregory green and small; if I'da known how to fuck at eighteen going home in a Studebaker; if you don't get a hard-on you get a price, I mean, really, I wish you guys would under two hundred for the whole thing. . . . Tuesday sleeps plush.

Spring coaster in the morning with this cooking and coughing in the kitchen, hand loader off in the van practicing the Now Profession and it's great for guns finger-writing the revelations with two kinds of eucalyptus in view, maybe four or five. The wind has died down using the banana instead of the leaf, us dads at lunch (well, I do have two sons) with whirling Leslies before dope, before anything, on the North Tower looking south captivated by the view *gyrating* in the strands. The memories flood back unable to keep my mind on the subject in Huntington Beach as a man learns to look into the eyes and as the mind jells on the subject, what is it?

Never known. Never seen. A never hear flight of swallows (gulp) unpromised, lost unfulfilled—a road in paradise filled with panting refugees gasping along: you can't look back for the unfolding book, page by page in a straight line: no corner stores in Southern California, wagons that never got pulled feel their oats here! Drop the tab in the milk barrel and the fleshy baroque will toodle on amid the ruins. Massive, shattering anal detonations! Take a shit every day to feel outstanding, better.

The fucking transition rots the gray matter into jelly slime-slime Möbius striptease churning up the gelatinous mass into a neverend sentence of captivity distilled to smog, grit, and fire engine red, hear ye a See Egg within the Arsenal, stainless steel guns laying it out note by note while harpists play, *inspired* to keep it up, keep your fucking pecker up! A good test only to be shot dead by some other glistening stainless steel madness for bedding services known to the unknown—last vantage, hunkered down in the Epic Opera done in soft light, slim girl adorned. I can't draw you anymore with the radio hissing at me like J. Edgar Hey! remember me? I'm the guy that bought.

(Beach derricks fresh air road trash entitled *Quickjoint Pulltop,* Ann looks O.K. but no racer up on blocks in the garage, those days are overdone in the afternoon sun with strange radio many moons ago just bordering on something grand. Grander in fact.)

A cream in this wind. Can we get it together? The open land seething with black oilcans riveted boldly to the walking beam. Oh, God! the majesty of these people at home with new sheets and potted plants turned back before your very eyes like living things. Please don't die, loosing a wife in these times makes small brass drawerpulls out of the varnish, husbanding clean clothes proudly hailing anything said before the fall, chuckling righteously, drunkenly, in fluent Arabic, running down the personnel in a beautiful, singular light. The Heurist shines. I've never known Paradise before; the last, the last temptation. Who is going to pick up on a percussive wave of fulfilled dreams? How much is my time worth? May I have ten minutes? Freedom? Listening to these breathless moments a monk in Nepal spins Buddha's Prayer with forced air heat, "Black beach bojum only fuck your best friends with spit and baby magic."

Undefined from the Caucasus of the Orient, thousands of years old floating down the Yangsee with Mao & Thou, quite a trio. The whirlwind by the door calling down economic failures one after the other. Yes, I am that man gleaning a bottle of green death, the black shadow so fast as to make everything penny-ante, but you can stand up to it with Asian Glory after four thousand years of toil. Now am I free? Possibly of heart failure.

(The old Arabs sheiking away like nothing happened and just *yesterday* I saw it happen.) Quite a sight someplace. Anyplace. The other fellow doesn't like Henny Youngman, well flog it in the pornos listening to the last grasp, man.

UNKNOWN TO MANKIND BY THE VERY NATURE OF ITS MAKEUP

Stupidity! write you fool, that there's not much time left. Gasping, gasping Pong. Get down to earth so that doing backflips for Christ's Sake is no problem. Diet will resist aging as the latest findings of medical science prove. Let's face it, nobody showed up. Nobody had time for righteousness, the judges are always on foreign soil, and nobody has time for Gorilla Warfare, either.

Superbland basking in SoCal with Thrills & Cascades is such innocence one after the other sound asleep. This small notebook not too much a dummy—but not *intended* at this time, a *glorious* thought. Going out fast with bullshit aside, nothing between us last scene struck and the secondhand scraping by, the music deteriorating and confidence wanes. Eat your heart out, baby. Only his pop was a crazy braggart sweeping up oak leaves, enormous valleys populated by giants swelling over the land ("Gimme a good cigar...") back East

(Blam!, crash...)

THE BOTTOM LINE

Annex "Hey!":
Speaking in tight, broken phrases the night passes into day and leaving for City's Center without a single masturbation. Wondering at the vast of it all here, in hot sunlight or morning shooting up on Ocusol & 20c bus rides with kids still skateboarding on clear plastic. Everybody is going to the beach by used car lots selling racers only, please. Dr. Glad, Chiropractor.

Comfort uncoming in this profane stucco nightmare, drizzling smoggy acid on marble tombstones crumbling quickly to dust and excited to get downtown with fresh hairspray glossy and hard. May I rest in that peace burning my olfactory to that dust believing it's just another way of thinking.

More skateboards—with a rider on Social Security, *East* Whittier, no less (Gold is just nibbling at it). A large crow in the middle of street pecking absently, unemployment agency—"All Jobs Free"—out of business, main street deserted of life at ten A.M. Boy, there sure are some old-time heartaches down here. Raw, and oozing Need, Hope, Desire, Christian Ladies all. And now they're asking me not to break the chain. Such enchantment.

"Crow Village" the Chicano watchword. Emblazened graffiti in bario-style lettering, sad-ass huge tremendous Chicano graffiti. "Bizzaarr Massage Parlour" driving the straights up the wall. "Pato

MY TRIP

Cowboy", "Bario Jardin", "La Termite", "Tony Smily Night Owls", "Consuelo Mouse" scrubbing the concrete banks of the dry Los Angeles River to get the writers off! Absurd Gorilla Warfare.

Please don't call the police, I'm harmless. A youth of the revolution caught up in some bad action yearning to leave burritoland. Salida Solament, Compadres.

Electronic joy machines beeping behind neopreen doors with zeroids fondling the sweaty tits made of metal, laconic epitomes gathered together as youth. "Hate the sin but love the sinner," Hollywood. North Hollywood Barris bodies junked behind chain-link fences, reminders of youth wasted inhaling the fiberglass fumes of expanding economies. The nickname of America spelled flaccidly on the road, chrome varnished with sweat in Sagistic Vista! The most photographed twenty acres in the history of western flicks. Hidden trails (just keep your shit off the toilet) beaconing like Ahab's arm, the grotesque adventureland nobody will see: high nets to keep the golfballs off new cars, industrial parks sinking at the rate of three inches a year. Exactly how much oil is pumped out. Xenia, Ohio, keeps popping up. As a voice at last only because it's so close to Easter, taxiing down the apron, getting to the runway in about nine hours, too late to take off. Goodbye Southern California, you have officially ended (to the only sorting out that remains, and it's going to be a bitch to those of us closed to an ointment).

The man driving is a left lane rider Cammarillo passing by. "Mo El" on a new place. Relax in the Salad Bowl @ 50c a line. Citizens Individual Storage agonizing bitter-sweet sandy, sandy beaches. Intoxicants forbidden—a slim and delicate kind of comfort denied by the overwhelming convention at the tressels just outside of Santa Claus, the kids surf along here approaching the pastures of heaven ("You gotta be introduced, I don't take nobody off the streets") codified into a respectable nomenclature $10.00 & up. And then that youth, raw, vegetable-like, leaning on the railing intent for foxy chicks unknown to God, even to themselves, the size of a button going to Cucamonga, it's a style. Maybe a dream come true but surely not denied the endless summer. Gypsywheels drives around with his dad three days and eight changes later still to be reckoned with, the fantasy Samurai with robe never parted always saying high, my trip to Southern California on a nine by twelve demo. Let them eat cake! Eminent Domain *dead ahead,* **gasping for breath but saying "The Cosmic Cliche" over and over.**

The mare just emptied her bladder with the mighty legions of the devil, walking into a trap: this was a long trip strewn with bones and children without fathers. No nesting boxes, just the lining scattered lightly about. The perfect union holding hands with the old man's folly.

A broadside accident in red light and then somebody copies it and you got Japanese spaghetti. I'm in big trouble, I just dropped a cigar in my lap: the thought my work was comedy but it's only humor.

The Yellow Book of Conversations

RUTH MOON KEMPHER

*"But how do I know what I think, until I see what I say?"—
Saul Bellow, Educational Channel 7, Jacksonville, Fla. Tuesday Night*

July something at La Cantina, fake wine casks on fake stone walls presumably the

—J&B like usual?

yes I said to Judy's question that dipped out of the air like the upsidedown hook interrogation mark the Spanish use hung there over the presumably real plastic, red upholstered faked Captain's chairs that usually only tourists, or lovers sit at

Albert. Battledor; shuttlecock; beetle bug. Albert scuttled in buggy into the dark barroom in his dark glasses. Convex? Concave? The lenses bulge ( ) like flies' eyes. Baggy black pants. Long dark hair thin and dirty, the hair and also Albert, who said without even hello

—o there you are Beth did you bring it today?

—She always brings it; said Simon Bolivar Cardenas who owns La Cantina and who was standing behind the bar looking at things and stroking his trim sleek black beard nervously as if he too was reminded by Albert of bugs.

—That's why I love her. Everywhere she goes, she brings it. I was sitting at the white formica top bar of course, trying to write a grocery list and I waved my pen at Albert behind me and said: It's on the table you just went past.

Albert swooped back and grabbed up the book. Bright pink jacket: *Candy*. —You remembered!

—Flea powder. I said that musingly. All the bugginess had reminded me. O, if I forget flea powder, the dogs will disown me.

And Sim laughed. —How come you're too cheap to buy a copy for yourself, Al?

Albert, already reading, never looked up from the page— O I can only read it in here. I know that. What if I passed away in an alcoholic stummer and they sent a book like this back to Mother

Albert they tell me was an Intelligence Officer in the war. The Big War. But I don't know

Judy bartends as flexible as if she were a rubber doll. The skin of her hand as she pours from a bottle looks that soft, like doll rubber. The long, tapered fingernails though, might be steel. She poked herself in the ribs as she shoved me my J&B on the rocks —You hear about last night, Lovie? No? You're the only one in town then. I been ribbed so much it's a wonder I got any left. Everybody comes in so smart and says, you goin' swimmin' again tonight, Judy? I was so embarrassed, I got right out of that damn pool and sat in his car. That cop, I don't know his name, he shined his light into the car and said O, it's you. I thought Jeez, I must have some reputation in this town. One of the other guys got this robe from a chair, and some guy hustled right out from one of the rooms and said: Hey how about giving me back my robe? I was glad I'd kept my dress on. That other guy hadn't. I called Sim I didn't want to come in today, I was that embarrassed but he made me. He said *face it*. But I was that embarrassed. He said: You get your ass in here in forty minutes. I was about an hour. You ever try to comb wet hair?

Albert —I want to ask you, Beth do you

Whatever he said, I sort of nodded because Judy saying *dress* had reminded me of what I'd dreamed last night. I was trying to find a new dress. But everything the saleslady showed me was ridiculously out of style, or too big, or coming apart at the seams. When I told her I'd like something like the dress I'd worn in, she looked at the label and sniffed: Humpf. They've even given you a false address.

Dress / address?

Albert, repeating, scowled his question from behind those dark green lenses —It's this New York Zen maybe? Different from California Zen?

and Dolly, Sim's sweet-faced, plump wife came back from the ladies' room, and sat herself beside me at the bar, whispering, or at least, speaking softly —Did Luis say anything to you about me and Sim?

—No. What about? Albert, I don't know one Zen from another

—o, I got mad and we were kind of split up for a while. Nobody much knew. But Luis was at the Lazy when I lit into Sim. He's back now. I guess he got sick at the Hotel. He couldn't find any blankets

Judy smiled pleasantly at Dolly and me. —I'm going to sue

the City I think or that guy the Manager, what's his name? I ought to write him a letter at least. I hit this lamppost a couple months back, you know? And anyway they just charged me three hundred fifty bucks

—For a lamppost?

Eyes opened wide.

—No, no. Well, yes. That's part of it but mainly fertilizer. And plants. It was twenty-five bucks for fertilizer, and fifty bucks for the forty hedge plants I hit before I got to the lamppost, and then that lamppost and a day and a half wages for putting it back. Well, I came around yesterday and looked at those new hedge plants

A big, heavyset man came in, fat, really, overhanging stomach and all. He ordered a Bud in a can when he found out they don't have draft. Then a friend of his came in and said right away: Goddamn it Ferrol, you hitting it this early again after last night?

—I learn from my mistakes, said the fat man with beer fuzz on his lip —I'm the only son of a bitch you know who'll admit it, too

they went off together, the fat guy carrying off the beer in one plump paw like he didn't even have to bend his fingers to hang on, it could be glued there

—well, all that fertilizer I paid for, and those hedges. That's why I ought to sue, I think. They look. Not so hot.

A woman wearing a heavy, musky perfume came in and sat at one of the back tables, Fay I think, chattering about how many martinis J. T. drank last night. The usual junk. Gobbledegook. Too many words —Sandy has a rude surprise in store for her. J. T. isn't going home.

Sim said, about his room at the hotel: the shower was so (with his hands, a rectangle) dinky, Beth I couldn't believe it. You couldn't turn your ass to the water

Albert who had put *Candy* down and gone, unnoticed, came back. —It really is going to rain. Beth, Lovie, couldn't you do something about this storm clouds and thunder business everyday?

Sim, mostly to himself —Next time I move out, it'll be the last

Everybody, including Dolly, said O Yeah. Sarcastically.

Postulate: A woman keeps a notebook, for a hobby, for a distraction, for an exercise in inhumanity, puts down conversations. Pretends to be doing a grocery list. 3 lbs hambg f freezer. Lean. If cheap. Soon she's so in to it, she's listening to everything, even the tiny sounds of perfume creeping in the air, for the notebook. Sifts the voices, too, yes. That's a good one, if I can just pen it here somewhere, among the eggs and bking potatos 10 lbs. Until the book becomes an obsession. Her entire life lived for and around the notebook's yellowbound pages. And when her psychiatrist finally finds the book, which would give him the key to her soul's heartsickness, the cure, he discovers he can't read her writing. Slow fade to black.

Albert, tapping *Candy* by my elbow with a chipped, extremely dirty fingernail —now is that Zen? Or just introductory? I feel I've been missing something here, for nine pages

J. T. came in and up to the bar, a slim curve-spined young

man in tired jeans, ordered a Bloody Mary and went back with it to sit with Fay or whoever that was, softly moaning

Judy —What's that woman's name, working for the *Record* now?

I — You mean Lee Something, Happyvale? Merryvale?

Albert, surprised —You know that woman? I met her once. It was midnight and I dropped by for a go-home shot and a beer and there sat this blob, in a dress, white and all. . . jet beads. What is it? Fringes. All beads in fringes, rows and rows and *rows* of fringes, just sitting there, *quivering*

Somebody put a quarter in the juke box tucked in under the fake barrels sticking out three inches with real spigots, but that three inches is all. *La Vie En Rose,* violins and piano, pianissimo, spun into the room, and I thought how odd, Piaf's song in a fake Spanish Cantina, fits

I shook my head —Never met her. But the first thing I read that she wrote, she started off with a triple negative. It got me on the spine. I'm not a purist, in the purest sense, but

Judy scowled at Albert —Don't let Beth kid you. She's awful smart. The phone rang, at the other end of the bar, and Judy moved, moltenly, to answer

My friend I sometimes call "The Prince of Jesters" came in and leaned by me, dressed in two shades of pale blue, white bucks, a perplexed expression, round face —Saw the Ford in the lot Sweetie and I just had to come by. That party Beth last night you wouldn't have believed it.

Judy, loudly, phone in her ear: Is J. T. here?

Everybody, a chorus, including J. T. at the back table: No!

—I'll never go there again, I swear it, even if he is my psychiatrist. He was dancing with Faith. You'd love Faith, but they got to rolling around on the carpet. Well I took little old me out on the balcony then, for a ciggy

—You want anything?

—What? O. No thank you. The bod couldn't stand a single shock more. But what was worse, Beth. From there, I went to She's, and her mother was there. You know. The Dragoness. Well, I didn't need that, either. A house full of hostile

Sim said —we're out of Hennessy (reflectively, listening)

—Two years ago, I swear, it would have thrown me into remission. No more. Have I told told you I saw Betty Sue? Honestly, it's sad. She used to be so terribly special to me, but now, Land, if I close my eyes, she could be any of these frumps. Sad. Their child is an angel. Aquarius, like you and me, so naturally. . . she took a bag of potato chips and dumped them on the floor, shook that bag and laughed. You've mortified your mother, I told her. —Can you say mortified? Mort, she said. Mort! Mort! O, she's a doll

Judy, who had been waiting, impatiently, to get her words in: I still want to know about the Merryvale chick. Is she married or what?

Albert—She told Sim that night I saw her, she had a husband in Connecticut and then next day she said California. I don't know. Maybe he moves around a lot.

Sim, pretending he hadn't clearly heard Judy ask my friend did he want a drink, asked, too.

—No no, he said, I just came in to tell Beth a thing or two. Beth Above Reproach. He chuckled, and waved, and was gone. (Beth Above Reproach, that's his name for me, but why...)

Beside me, Dolly had turned to tell René of the Patisserie how Sim had gotten sick at the hotel and had to come home and René was waving his hands and trying to tell her about his troubles with the Restoration people, and their building codes for San Agustin Antigua —He tells me I haff to haf the. You know my display case? I haff to haf the back-ree in the blue building and the res'trant in the yellow one. Now I know. My contract say. They can help with the decor, but not

and what I wrote down, carefully, was: tuna fish, 3, if f/$1. still.

but what I was thinking was of was last Sunday, when the Prince of Jesters and Beth Above Reproach and Beth's husband Jonah had been sitting on the deck at our hourse, looking out over the chill blue rolling in ocean, pelicans going past single file, flying a dipping line, taking advantage of heat thermals, coasting, huge wings spread and I was telling them both about Francie, who works as a secretary where Jonah works, and how I'd met her on King Street in front of the 5 & 10, how I'd hung on to a lamppost while she told me all this garbage, lovely sungold, bluesky day, explaining to me all about what I might be hearing about her and Jonah, how it's all the product of idle minds, quoting to them, over our rum and tonics, what Francie'd said, that was already in the notebook —we work together but nothing more, you know. Kid around a lot. You know how Jonah is. (I ought to, swinging on my lamppost, after all these years.) If there had been, we were sure being damned open about it. Ha ha. It's a good thing my man and you both know what's going on.

Nothing. Somebody could be killed, otherwise. It's terrible. One of the drivers wanted me to go out for a drink with him. I'd have liked to. Means nothing, but I'd have enjoyed it, to relax a little. It's a group, he told me, Who could it hurt? —Group, schmoop, I said, That don't matter. I've got to live in this town a long time, I hope.

I like *La Vie en Rose* . . . if there were words with the music now, we'd be circling again, to *Hold me close, and hold me fast, the magic spell you cast. . .*

—But Beth, let me tell you what Marlo said to me about Fay: Don't you know she's runnin' around? Well she is, and I know it well as anybody, but I said to her: How could Fay be running around? She has all those skads of kids. . .

and there was Fay, I think, didn't want to look, behind at that table, with J. T. Albert had carried his beer over there and was saying, who probably never had a wife, himself, J. T. You've got to see Sandy's position, she's stuck at home all the time with those kids, and

and there are so many fish out there beyond our house, in the ocean in our yard, it's incredible, probably have even our own tuna

Jonah was squinting in the reflection off the seaoats, the dunes' sand, or else he was just peeved at what I'd repeated of the lamppost-in-sun-with-Francie conversation. A look of disgust, or sun pain. —It's Marlo that's doing the running around, he said. —She's cock happy. When she meets a man for the first time, the first thing she looks at is his feet. I thought about how funny our Prince had looked, half in jest and half appalled at Jonah's choice of words, me thinking it's a banner day for the notebook, if I can pop in this string, word on word

La Vie en Rose had ended, and now Ella Fitzgerald was singing from a scratchy, old record, "On my own, would I wander through this Wonderland alone," Curiouser and curiouser...

—His feet? I remember prompting, question for more and more —Why would she look at a man's feet?

Jonah: Umm, well. That's supposed to show, in proportion, the length of everything else. If you've got say, size 5 feet, well that's small for a man, but it's okay, if you're a little man. But if you're six feet tall, man, you better wear size 13's or Marlo won't look again. She figures on all that and keeps lookin'. She says it's okay to drive a Chevvie if that's all you can get, but if you can find a Ferrari, well

later on, he handed me the binoculars —Look at this nut down on the beach. He's got a flowered bathing suit on, with suspenders, to hold it up

o, that was a banner notebook day. "Too misty," sang Ella. "Too much in love..."

and some kook down at the other end of the bar suddenly looked up from his drink and said —Lemme tell you guys a joke, okay? You all know why a Jew can't play golf?

René had turned from Dolly to me, waving his hands, excitement in every finger. —O Beth. I found a raf-france for the umbrellas. Not a good raf-france, but for the shit-ass Historical Commissioners you should not mind the expressing, this is a Goddamn sit-seatuation. I don' wan' vines. It will ran, you know? And then they will be dripping ran. Tha's all right for a house in a magazine maybe, but problems. Well, I weel haff problems with the bugs outside anyway. Do I need it inside, too?

—Is Merryvale a made-up name, Beth?

—A pseudonym?

—No, I mean, is it real?

Dolly had a friend beside her, too, somebody putting in a pitch for the bartender out at the Breakwater Bar on the beach, wants to change jobs

Dolly, sweet as always, smiled. Can turn off anybody without their knowing —He may be all right as a bartender, but for me, he lacks a lot of cooth

I ordered another drink, in the interim

Dolly's blue eyes smiled deeper, as my bill grew —We aren't hiring anybody now, anyhow. She was laughing at my growing grocery list, too —I don't think you'll make it there

I took my fresh drink from Judy —I'm just getting ready, is all. Got to be primed up for the assault on the canned goods, so I don't wilt in the Meat Department

Judy giggled, as if I'd said something vaguely obscene

—Because he can't yell 'Fore!'

René was paying his bill. I wished him luck with the Commissioners.

—Thanks vaar much. I will need that.

I thought about the last time I'd been to the store. A wasted day. Constipation of the soul. Went to Wynn-Dixie for 10 lbs of potatoes and 2 cucumbers and 4 green bell peppers, and still with only that and a *TV Guide* had to wait 10 minutes in line.

Lettuce (who bowls against La Cantina [Dolly and me and others] for the Chevrolet Place, a friendly team to bowl against, except we always try to win) said —If it'd been me, I'd have decided to have some other kind of potat. Of salad

—O? O. You mean the wait in line. Well, that's nothing. Besides this, I went around the post office seven times, to park. The town's swarming with people, tourists. . .

Lettice: This just isn't your day, I guess

(and I decided she obviously thought I really only went through all this torment, like the descent into Hell, for Jonah's salad? no, for another Make Money Envelope, which I didn't hesitate however, to pick up. Actually, it was the second time I'd gone in for little stuff I might otherwise have let slide until the big shopping, regular, Wednesday, so maybe she's right. Greed. Avarice. Ten million other sane adults right now standing in Wynn-Dixie lines, confidently looking for the right-hand half of the thousand dollar bill)

—Because he has to yell Three ninety-eight!

Dolly sort of snickered at the joke, but I who sometimes think of my unknown grandmother and grandfather the Rabbi and Uncle Ike and all, decently (besides, it was a bad joke) abstained.

Dolly told me: They're having a Special on prime ribs at Pantry Pride. Saw it in last night's *Record*

Observation: A woman with the habit of word-snatching. Discovers sentences are just like tuna fish. Ah, the bigger ones

THE YELLOW BOOK

that slip away. Dreams of long, glistening, finny words in schools. Discovers (too late) her mistake. They aren't fish at all, but fluid. Goggles as she drowns.

—Prime ribs?

I thought of Eve, sadly. Said.

—I can't afford the gas to travel that far over town.

> This is the first chapter from
> *The Yellow Book of Conversations*

from Words From Xibala

HUGH FOX

The swing in the willow swung out over the pond. Her daughter couldn't swim, she almost cut the ropes through and when they broke and she fell in the water and almost made it to shore she put her foot on her daughter's head—careful, careful not to touch her face—and held her under.

Six weeks on the road. He came in, the house seemed deserted. Incense coming from upstairs. He opened the bedroom door, she was sitting in the bed propped up, surrounded by pillows, all pink and gold and perfect, and it wasn't until he'd touched her cold face that he saw that the eyes weren't really inside the eyesockets, that there were other lips under her lips saying,

"Won't I do now?"

XXX

Neither of them had intended it. They'd both been out drinking, both had been stopped before "coming," fucking Turd Puritans, then back home, hot, night, their parents upstairs, hair, sweat, perfume, it had happened, when she woke up two hours later in his room and "saw" what she'd done, she got up and took her butane lighter, set the curtains on fire, threw aromatic lamp oil all over the rug, watched the fire spurt, grow . . . he woke up, she was sitting watching the fire.

"Come on." He grabbed her, upstairs to warn their parents. Door locked. Seemed like they'd never wake up. Smoke all over now. Then his mother opened the door.

"The goddam house is on fire."

Couldn't go back down the stairs now. Father up. "How did it get started?"

Out through the window, a little "ledge" on the roof and then a huge old willow just up against the house, a heavy elephant trunk branch out over the "ledge."

"Don't look down," the son said as his sister started out on the branch, then his mother, his father, himself.

"Look, it's coming up through the roof," said the sister, looking down, the branch broke and they all fell down three stories to the concrete driveway.

XXX

Desert, alone.

"Come on in," the voice said.

He looked down at the small spineless cactus, small opening in the middle, thought *too small* as it expanded, grew, he walked in through the opening, found himself in a huge underground cone-room and at the very bottom, the sun had begun to rise up through the floor.

Scenes from the Thistledown Theatre

IRENE MUSILLO MITCHELL

Weltschmerz and the Boy

It was spring's human hand caressing her face, fondling her hair that disturbed. Winter's piled snows had locked memories and old wounds; she had been austere and preserved like an arctic zone. But this south wind infected like a pathology. Yes, spring was a vulnerability, a breaking into feeling. It was a new port of call, a country of gnawing sensibilities.

She felt lonely, an existential loneliness, a weltschmerz. Middle aged, within, the folding of wings, the gathering of silences, the principle of spring could not be addressed to her. There was a black-winged irreversibility between her and the cherry blossom air, between her and the innocence of these first blue hyacinths.

Nothing, no one could console. In eyes everywhere she saw extinguished dawns; in hands gesturing or still, formulations of deep, primal desertion.

Then she saw Charles her eight-year-old playing "Trucks" in the small dirt pile on the meadow, his straight blond hair over his eyes. She knew his hand accompanied by proper acoustics from his voice was guiding a Matchbox truck around roads meticulously built; she knew he was following the classic dictates of the game: in snowtime the truck must slip on ice and go off the road; in nonsnow it must get stuck in mud; there must always be occasion for the tow truck; and there must always be occasion for trucks or cars to "peel off," leaving convulsive marks on dirt or part of tires on asphalt.

Charles! the mode of the child, his ease in nature, his trustful gaze at the giant maple, bare, leafing, turning in autumn; his unity of self like a bright integer amidst irreconcilable dualities. He must walk with her; they must walk together through the pines down to the stream.

But would he? Of course, he would have to park his truck: in whatever urgency—including bedtime—he could no more break the integrity of the game than a rushed artist could leave colors or lines out of a painting. And usually parking was complicated, entailing not only repeated movements in drive and reverse (with acoustics) but prior to this a professional determination of the proper spot. . . . And there was Tommy who might come to play with him.

She walked across the meadow, heard the casualness of her voice as she addressed him, and saw the far blue eyes gazing at her from the distances of childhood. She heard her voice again . . . the snowy owl. No, that was a blunder—who would see a snowy owl now?

She barely heard his slow, awkward reply, barely heard trucks, Tommy. A negative had entered his eyes; he did not want to go! She heard his "if you want me to go. . . ." But it was his wholeness, his inner truth she needed. Suddenly, she did not want to go. And then she saw Tommy—"But you will go, won't you," Charles was saying. Oh, certainly, she would go.

He stood waiting. She started across the meadow, turned;

he was still standing there, watching; he waved. She waved and walked towards the pines.

Return to the Childhood Locus

She stood at the corner of the city block. There, both sides the wide street were the two-family houses, each diverse in brick or stucco, one shingled. Of course, every vacant lot had since been built upon, and visible from the next block were apartment houses. But only six houses on one side and seven on the other were significant; only they stood within the glowing dimensions of memory and dream; only they were pervaded with a metaphysical mortar that rendered their substance as intangible as it was solid, as far, rainbow-hued as it was approximate and commonplace. In particular, the sixth house down from the corner where she stood (she could not see it): brick, porches on first and second floors, the former leading through two thick pillars into another, outer porch; there, up the concrete staircase onto the first floor where she lived ten childhood-through-adolescent years was the locus that had fastened onto her psyche with the sphinx-strange truths of myth.

Three hundred miles, a costly train fare, excuses to return to the city to replenish supplies; then two subways and a bus to stand here. It did not matter that she had lived in other parts of the country; that she had married, had children, had arrived at middle age; that the whole context of her life was different: How could that noble yet baroque immigrant household live in her now? How could that furniture, that wallpaper; the Latinate Christmases and the strange Mediterranean admixture of severity and lyricism claim her who had graduated to a different order of tastes. Nonetheless, in dreams night after night she was here. And now, more than twenty years later, here she returned.

She must walk casually down the block, not too fast, not too slow—walk this very sidewalk she would run up on summer evenings to kiss her father coming home from work, hold his hand, and walk home together to dinner. Now she must slow her pace; she was coming to the stucco house where her Polish friend used to live. (A man walking a dog was coming towards her. He passed.) Here at the side of the house was the passage leading to the back gate, which she would open, and then standing in the yard, call, Natalie! Natalie! She laughed at this childhood figure, even loved her maternally; she remembered Junior, the bully, and herself incensed calling beneath his windows, Junior's mother! Junior's mother!

But now she was approaching—suddenly, children ran out of a yard and started a game on the sidewalk close by. One more house and—here! here it was. She must look at it—no, not look but with a North Star fixity, an archintelligence penetrate this solidity to the weightless, translucent structure of her dreams, where she still lived. Was it not recently she was sleeping again in her childhood bedroom—that very room there that gives with two windows onto the porch (on sleepless nights, she would imagine she saw a shadow on the window shades)—but instead of her sister, her youngest child was sleeping in the other bed.

She must touch this brick, which in her dream was curiously liquid and suffused with light, an acute material vibrant with the bright-condensed, symptomatic logic of the psyche.

She pretended to drop something, moved closer to the house, and put one foot on the first step of that concrete staircase where her father had stood, hands over eyes, when he learned of the death of his mother 3,000 miles away; that staircase that had supported the still-less, sun-flickering aspen feet of childhood and a first pair of silk stockings as exotic and aromatic as perfumes and spices from the East; the staircase that like wise, metamorphosed fairy tales had been an intermediary between the patriarchal indoors and the measureless principles of the outer world, instilling incredible wisdom in childhood eyes.

But she was lingering too long. The children had stopped playing and were watching her. She smiled at them and continued down the block. And although she knew within days she would be here again in dream, she wept, weepless. She wept for the child that had been; she wept for the father that was dead. She wept for the far, nameless loneliness that had brought her here, that now returned with her on bus, on subway, on a train speeding 300 miles away.

The Woman in the Laundromat

Fels, Non-Polluting Laundry Detergent, Clorox; three boxes of clothes—four o'clock; she would be here till six. One must dispose dry and efficiently with such chores, with long-accustomed economy of thought and movement. In fact, one must almost not be there; one must fight continually the gargantuan appetite of *domesticus*, which feeds on women's brains and energies; one must preserve oneself for—for this volume of poetry, for example, under fifty dirty socks.

Quickly, sort whites and colors; quickly, throw them into the impassive machine, which hopefully upon ingesting two quarters will set its metallic digestion in motion; soap, extra Clorox certain to clean—if calamitously—the clothes; and now, poetry.

"Good-by, Lorry," someone said. She looked up from her book at "Lorry." Lorry waved and continued an apparent arbitration before three stepladder children: Now it was Jane's turn; then it would be Diana's. She seemed goodhearted, fair; the children appeared healthy and reasonably, tumbingly smudged. She rose to insert a dime in the dryer. She was fleshy and vague like cells that had lost some long-ago motivation lapsing into shapelessness. A symptomatic incoherence rested unopposed upon her face, and the dandruff-specked jersey and lax gesture exuded an imminence of slovenliness. . . . Yes, she was a victim; something critical in her had been eaten up.

Of course, women succumbed in various ways. Many, strong-minded and organized, sated *domesticus* by assimilating it, making it not a means but an end. They, too, had been eaten, but they possessed purpose, method, a commendable intelligence.

But Lorry . . . one could imagine the sad, irredeemable succession of hours reduced only to straggly, deep-stained chores: dishes into the next meal; disorderly rooms still disorderly, recalling a first elan of housekeeping; the continual children—and spilt milk; if nothing else, the indomitable elemental dirt of existence: what shoes bring in; what clings to the pile of coats; hair! maddeningly omnipresent and unriddable; the vitality of pores! oils, sweat, even celestial acids from children's bodies—whole days, whole years of turbid domestic inundation, of nonmind; a gestalt sans concept, sans category, like a thick, sprawling, unsavory gravy.

It was a relief to look away from Lorry at the book of poetry, the precise fixing of thought, the neat divisions into stanzas. Almost half-past four: the clothes must still be put into dryers and then folded. Of course, folding must be quick, economical of concentration—if the four corners of sheets did not meet in all their multiples, what of it? If the king-size sheet were slightly bunched somewhere in its folds, it would be pressed in the linen closet, and besides, it would be on the bed in six days. After all, cleanliness was the first honesty. And given today's crease-resistance—more or less—even casual shirts and blouses folded hastily and pressed in bureaus sat reasonably well on the body—or in any case, the modern unstarched eye preferred a natural look. . . . If she folded this way, how would Lorry fold—or would she?

In fact, at this moment Lorry was folding clothes: a pillow case—she flapped it, then lengthwise corner to corner, laid it down, smoothed it, folded, another fold, smoothed—a perfect rectangle any mathematician could apply a compass to; other pillow cases; now sheets criminal to unfold for future use; children's blouses (destined for immediate crumpling and spilt milk), collars and sleeves professionally manipulated; and on the table a slow mounting of categories of clothes like axioms.

Lorry's face was absorbed, intent upon this act of structuring reality into clean, bright arrangements. The blank spaces and succumbed features of her face transmuted into a definition of person. Some potential in her inferred itself through the positive movements and unproblematic completion of each folding. Perhaps it responded to the soap-smelling cleanliness of the materials of this experience; perhaps it was grateful for a chore that implied the satisfactions of form; a definite beginning, a logic of procedure, finis and concomitant perception of achievement.

Accidentally, one of the children upset a stack, and although Lorry had almost finished and must remove the clothes into her laundry basket, she straightened the stack and patted down the collar.

The Finger

ARTHUR WINFIELD KNIGHT

Always late and breathless, standing in the doorway to the classroom as if he had run from somewhere so far that he couldn't make it till the latebell rang and I was hanging out the slip of paper with the names of the absent students. It was hopeless calling out his name when I took roll because he wouldn't be there, just as it was hopeless writing down his name as absent since he'd be there by the time I hung the slip out. Always late because he'd take a final drag on his cigarette while he came across the lawn in the langour and lentitude of highschool spring.

When he was late, he'd run. Not because he wanted to get to a class on time, but because he needed to make a show, as if he'd be admired for the way he came in with his long hair hanging down across his forehead, wearing levis and a button-down shirt. So cool. Standing there. When he'd rather be out with his old 12 gauge, sighting a pheasant as it sloped into his sights and then . . . the slow slow squeeze to a feathery flight to death in a ditch. His old bitch of a pointer going out to retrieve.

Dan didn't want to be in school except for the weekend dances or the big Friday night football games of highschool America where the cheerleaders all jump with the flash of their white white thighs under the lights in a small town with the roar of old Chevy mufflers after the game at rootbeer stands and cold hotdogs at the game itself and beer and quick dark sex in backseats, all confused.

Almost all the students' parents worked in the big Kimberly-Clark plant doing whatever it was they did in a place like that, which was the only source of employment in town, except for the pharmacy and Safeway store. And a bar. Just a small town that was divided by 99—no more than a blur of pink and chartreuse to those who drove thru, the highway dividing and hiding the ugliness. Keep the kids off the street during the day and night when the moon tries to shine down thru the trees and students are stopped by cops for just walking along as if the country's no longer free. And it's not. All of us living and dying with the slow dull pain no anodyne can cure.

Dan trying to struggle and sweat thru the lessons I had to teach (because the principal believed that grammar was good for the mind, a skill needed to write) and no one cared. Even I didn't know the answers, looking them up in a manual that came with the book. Students should write about the way they feel when they're fucking or the way they come to games drunk even though they're not supposed to, just as they are not supposed to smoke or swear or go off hunting on a school day or the way they're not supposed to walk along the roads at midnight even though they all do some things that they're not supposed to, just as we did and we probably should have—I took wild highschool rides with a friend in the afternoon, and we'd both get drunk—when one beer fizzled on the carseat, I just held it out the window though I knew I'd be arrested—but I wasn't—piling beer cans on the coffee table with a student whose mother was the head of the English department at the elementary school—she'd told me how glad she was that I'd come to teach (the past and present) tearing up his paper since he wrote a theme describing going to the whorehouse after he'd read Steinbeck—but he'd taped it together, turning it in. To receive an A.

The principal thought he knew what he was doing because his undergraduate degree was in English, and the chairman had

THE FINGER

majored in math, with a minor in physical ed; how he came to be the head of the department or even to teach English the way he did, having kids diagram impossible sentences with fifty words or more (just like this) I never knew . . . . Incredible lies and hassles caused by parents who accused me of teaching fornication in class—one saying I'd asked a married senior named Ken how many times he and his wife made love, and the man who'd called was worried that his daughters might have to take my class; although he didn't know who'd told him the rumor. He couldn't tell Ken or me when we drove to his place at the edge of town. In the late morning light. The principal had called me into his office and then he'd called Ken. Since he hadn't bothered to check with him first. The way things were run. Ken came in and denied it. One of the few truthful people I met—a D student who was very sincere and a good person to be with that morning when we drove out to ask the guy why he'd lied. Or hadn't bothered to check the facts. He just stared at us thru the old screen door that looked like it was ready to fall off its hinges onto the rotting wood of the porch. Chickens ran thru the ochre dust. When we left, Ken and I took our time driving around because neither of us wanted to be in class, and we were both excused. So we smoked and joked—no school for awhile.

Dan also doing D work—uncaring, as long as he passed. No grade was too low but an F, although I never knew if Dan or the others would care if they flunked; or if they'd just be deprived of whatever pitiful thing they'd get—a new used car for the degree their parents didn't possess. Dan was taking 11th grade English for the second time.

All of the kids with bad reputations wanting to prove they were tough, lounging in the back of the room the first day or two, near the windows where the books were stacked. The person who'd taught my classes the year before was older. A woman who'd finally quit in the last couple of weeks because they'd lock her out of the room while they threw out books, shot craps and threatened: We'll break your arm. Or said she'd be raped. What a bunch.

I moved the worst into the front row and gave them extra assignments every time they caused any trouble; and they didn't like sitting there. Dan was supposed to sit in front of my desk, but one morning he walked toward the back, sitting there.

"Take your seat."

He just shook his head.

"You're sure?"

"Yeah."

"That's your final decision?"

"Yeah. What'll you do, beat me up?"

"I don't know. But I don't think you'll like it."

"Tough shit."

"OK." I got up from my desk and just stood there looking at him sitting in the wrong seat in the back of the room and I really didn't know what to do, because I wasn't allowed to hit him and even if I were, I know I could never win in a fight. So I just kept looking at him while he looked at the floor and the class watched me. Finally I went to the door because the principal's office was fifty yards or so from my room. "I'll be back."

"I can't wait."

The principal and the dean of boys were standing over near the administration office and I just asked the dean to come over since he'd had trouble with Dan before. When I'd explained what had happened, Frank just opened the door to my room and said: "Dan, pick up your books," while he waited to see if Dan would obey. And he did. Coming slowly over to where we stood. Then Frank told him: "You're out of school for two weeks. And come back with your parents."

"They work—"

"You should have thought of that before."

THE FINGER

Mr. Leffler came over too, and told Dan that he could memorize the Gettysburg Address and recite it when he returned with his parents, and that he wouldn't be in my class anymore. He could finish out the year with Mrs. Lane, who'd been the one to flunk him before.

Probably not minding the fact that he wouldn't have to be in school for two weeks because he could sleep late every morning—unless he wanted to go off with his gun or maybe fish or just goop around the smalltown pinball machines where the punks always hang out (and I did too when I was young) tilting the machine and hoping that the big TILT light wouldn't flash on—with nothing to do but play all day or watch inane serials about the dreariness of life (no worse than his own) on TV and, ah shit, who cares? Listening to his old man and woman bicker and bitch and unwind at night—or in the early morning, depending on which shift they worked, making toilet paper or whatever it was they did—with gigantic 16 ounce cans of beer being consumed. Sometime he'd probably study the Gettysburg Address (maybe the day before he was supposed to come back) but he'd somehow stumble

Four score and seven years ago

thru that and the only bad thing was the boredom that he had to get thru with his friends in school all day and the cathode ray of TV and crazy TILT lights in the downtown gloom of poolrooms that everyone knows. And missing the big Friday night football games that he couldn't attend. While he was out of school. But getting drunk with a bunch of his friends, he showed up the first Friday night and when Frank Robinson wouldn't let him in at the gate, Dan cussed him out. Then swung. A heavy fist coming toward Frank, who'd been a boxer in college and just blocked the blow before he hit Dan once in self-defense, probably glad he'd swung, and broke his nose. Flattening him there in the dirt with the lights of the stadium shining down on Dan while he lay there in a mass of cups and papers with his bloody nose. All of the kids kept going past to the game.

Coming into Leffler's office with his parents who talked about suing the dean (but never did) and probably ended-up beating Dan because he'd lost or because they'd missed time at work while they listened to the principal talk about Dan's problems and Dan mumbling

> our fathers brought forth on this continent

or something that resembled the Gettysburg Address even if it wasn't quite correct. Good enough. A sad working couple—oh Jesus life is dreary, what a drag sitting there.

Lillian Lane told me that Dan never caused any trouble once he'd come into her class, and when I saw him between one of the three-minute breaks where students rushed from one room to another and I rushed into the little humid boiler room next door to my classroom where I'd smoke a cigarette and talk to the geography teacher who always smoked part of a fat cigar since we had to hide while we smoked because we were supposed to set a good example, as if students didn't think we were human, Dan came up and said he was sorry, and I told him it was alright. Since it was. No worse than all the rest, he just happened to be the one who had to try me.

When Mr. Leffler was driving home he saw a group of kids on the corner and one of them gave him the finger. Dan. At least that's what the principal said. Although Dan denied it, he was expelled.

Coming into my room the last day on campus, and saying: "I'm going to a good school. Gettin' out of this hole."

"Good luck."

"Yeah."

"I mean it." And did. Wondering if he'd ever graduate and

THE FINGER

what would happen to him, this person I hardly knew whose life was so incredibly complex that I could talk to him for a week or more and have him in class, looking up all his records and his IQ, and never know who he was. Somehow seeing him forlornly walking thru fields where hyssop grew with the scent of its leaves in the blue—Dan walking along with his old bitch of a dog and his 12-gauge gun tucked into the crook of his arm, walking as if he had purpose that was somehow more important or beyond that of the hunter as a pheasant flew before him and he raised the gun that glinted in the early morning sunlight and the bird fell, just as Dan had somehow in a way that no one, even Dan, could ever fully fathom as he pulled the trigger— not just lost to those he'd left in moving (all of us who'd never known him) but a lonely, dark and sullen figure trudging thru the thistle toward the bird.

Insert: On Saying Goodbye

GIORGIO MANGANELLI

Translated from his HILAROTRAGOEDIA *from the Italian by W. S. Di Piero*

Saying goodbye, like suffering, has various qualities, here considered separately:

1) extrinsic

This type is revealed in ritually defined, symbolic gestures whose resonance is therefore cavernous, disproportioned, and ludicrous as well. Departures, then, a sign of symbolic dread. Take train departures, a symbol of all that passes, of decease, disappearance, non-being, never-being-born: it entails the deafening racket of bickering limbs, scalp eversions, in a place packed with serious, sordid, and insolent porters, newsboy nuncios of enchanting disasters, pompous admirals of the rails, commodores of luggage. A tragic and undignified place, bucked up by a whiff of infants' piss, swarming sobs all dressed in striped sweaters; reeking with the pathos of hairy, moaning sex (lovers are always, *always,* separating); epilepsy of handkerchiefs, spastic explosions of hands and fingers cracking their goodbyes: allusive confusion of timetables, changeovers, late arrivals, departure and arrival platforms switched around; shuffling body-fat, Grandmother's buttocks flogged by the loudspeaker's local dialect.

To say goodbye and say it well, the following is recommended: a day of wild and unlikely confusion, so that one's sadness gets poked by an elbow; deafened and abused by everyone else's hurried sorrows; cold sweats, calloused heartbreaks, quarrels, slobbering. So saying goodbye is finally a rite, insincere (even if you die of its pain when you get home, it'll still be insincere), clumsy, a poor show, crude (indeed downright coarse), incomplete, insulting, distracted (oh you'll die of it, you'll die of it)—and in the end the beloved person wrinkles, puckers, shrinks, turns into a foetus (dressed in rose garments), doubles back on its own conception and finally disappears in an air of foul words, obscenities, screaming sexual allusions, all light halved, infants' mucus, loosened neckties, cries of station-masters, windows whipping by with people on their way to the toilet. A spiritual exercise, the first stage of goodbye.

Or take a funeral. A human thing is being brought to its horizontal decomposition in that special hole—some mistake—anybody—cheap word: *body*—wildly inappropriate term—implicitly a *quodlibet;* the consanguineous flies, swarming and affectionate, cluster around the putrefaction, flesh free from the ignominy of sex, refused favors, ideological disorientation: they rush to enjoy the goodbye symbol easiest to handle—still no more than a symbol. There's a lot of hidden happiness at a funeral. You would be amazed to learn how much the son's solicitous hatred contributes to the dismantling of one's arms and legs; how attentively the clever wife with her dainty hands has worked at unstitching her ready-made and poorly-seamed *vir;* how, too, the nondead exult in having evaded their taxes . . . nixonites all . . . how they've parried the fatal and feather-light backhand slap. A mysterious, inarticulate joy felt even by the most loving, even by the most adjacent.

A funeral is allusive. Its foul presence throbs, an anonymous monster, lethal to this fragile continuity of ours. You move to the second stage of saying goodbye: speaking in a low but audible voice, you stand near the canned man, sniffing his inflorescence, shuffling your feet, you make a show of wanting to go up alongside him, to hold him back, but what you really do is follow him so that he can drink it in, soak it all up, soil himself, feast on his own special kind of goodbye; then once satisfied, he can settle down and forget us; he refuses to play cards with us, that beast imitating our father, that asthma cowering in the dark, he leaves us to our series of quick evenings, our temporary sleep.

Or take the migrant's goodbye, or the cuckold's. Such peculiar suffering, divorcing itself from its own misery, non-liberty, estrangement, betrayal, religion, bier . . . it glosses itself . . . treasured things we leave around so that we can hate them. Then too, fixed and prolonged suffering is good for continuity; but then again, maybe the only suitable dialogue is one with the hated beloved. A prison, an unfaithful woman, or a ruined chair—*that's* where imperfect divinity abides, or perhaps the most perfect, inaccessible to us.

Gloss on the unfaithful woman:

That she embody or act out a certain function of the divine seems obvious, and a demonstration of this is now in order. To raise her to the level of the divine you need only love her, with that muzzling devotion offered only to things we know are transitory and fraudulent. The mocking woman hovers above you, naked in her lower-worldly levitation.

Worship the flower of her cunt, compose liturgies, organise processions and *tridui* of that devout throng of your sex—muscles, groin, foreskin, drawn up in columns of sexual supplication, the fluttering of pious testicles beneath their scrotal canopies, behind the vulva-tabernacle.

Deceptive divinity—the only kind possible. Capricious, disloyal, inconstant, ignorant of itself, requiring propitiations of blood and sperm, devotional exercises of insomnia and sperm, the monotony of lamentations and sperm. Being a god requires inhumanity. God co-abides with the cloven-hoofed goat. . . . Smell his matted, senile whiskers. . . . Do you understand?

The female throbs with quintessential faithlessness. Hence the freedom of the divine. She accepts absences, approves of them, alters them. She who once drove you to supplication by swaying her buttocks now protests, protects herself, then consents, convincing you of her sincerity by glueing her sticky body to you, with the heavy presence of saliva and casual, lascivious fingering. Once trapped, you consecrate yourself as her sacrificial Host, and that's when she starts being unfaithful to you. That's when her thighs will clamp around other prey, other tithes, other regales.

And so, in your soul's perfect night, in the mincing lies of your parched and resonant brain . . . what's your verdict? What's your conclusion, cuckold?

Order of the day: to die, to kill, to sink like a submarine captain (hand on your visor, stifling your last belch) in a second-rate seacoffin. Solitude quickens the soul's karyokinesis. You sweat miserably (not unusual, but not inevitable) for those who suffer—a modest corporal phosphorescence. Foetus or neoplasm, the ectophotosphere coagulates into an image of an unsexed female, no pubes . . . breathless mouth, silence of the barren vagina, the scalding of the invading and charitable hand. You, cuckold, the most ludicrous of men, farce and mockery, you sprout a nail amid the slime of your censured sex, a lunulate feminine friend.

So: a wicked woman is herself a fraudulent divinity: she she humbles herself like a sacrificial *vas*, she becomes your handmaiden and martyr, the lustful turns lamblike, freshly cooked for your daily nutrition.

You'll eat your memory of her. Once she's lost her name, been mineralized like a haloed stegosaurus fossil, you'll then try to earn her forgiveness, you'll throb with gratitude for her infidelity.

So bend your knee, you who were born impure from her stammering womb—(it's the only way she could produce you)—bow to Her, the Fecund, the Fleshy, the Necessary.

Thus the unfaithful female, minister and whore, sets her own stake aflame.

And you, friend, burn her.

You, cuckold, love her.

Gloss on abandoning an uncongenial house:

You would think that the house under discussion, either because it's a mineral bed of memories or because it has symbolic value, would sadden the person about to abandon it . . . what with the cesspool, prison, and family group . . . horrible. Still, it's very painful to leave it. Look at any one of these wretched objects: a wardrobe with a rose-patterned cloth, a chair with its chintzy vegetable beauty, a place to put your ass—anonymous, unnamed, unbaptized stuff. There are thousands of wardrobes and chairs just like these. Would you say that this sickly, craven, deformed thing might act as a divinity? I say it *does*. And that inside its worm-eaten ramshackle wood there's a soul able to give life and death? That's *precisely* what I mean. These things are angelic and diabolical; man realized he's an exile among them; desiring sacred documents, he fumbled around those spaces between objects, then, dismayed and compelled, he raised his eyes and examined the roses, prostrated himself at the foot of the chair, begged absolution from a drawer. *But, you might reply, such things aren't congenial; they're awkward, ugly, inefficient.* Awkward, ugly, inefficient—such adjectives for divinity! *Awkward:* fitting you like a sweater ten times too large, with sleeves two sizes too short; *ugly:* because it's cluttered up the facial spheroid with an arrogant nose, damp optic caverns dribbling with lacrimose algae, impetuous too, the indiscretion of having made us in its likeness; *inefficient:* worse, lazy, puzzled, deafened by the rusted heavenly spheres. Oblivious to the universe it created, it draws close to the end of the world, then shakes the hairy cornucopia of the ear to make sure the first blasts of the trumpet can be heard. Then it goes back to sleep.

Correlary hypothesis of the preceeding gloss:

If this argument has a rational *quid*, then it lends credence to another hypothesis: that objects are not just an inhuman presence, as opposed to human, but *anti-human*. A coagulum of pain, as we can see, or rather as polyvinyl conglomerates (see above) of the Death-God's granules of despair; or chunks of fat cut from sorrow's obesity persuaded by the pressure applied by demiurgic thumbs to be born a tree (its vocation to be a bier or gibbet), or something metallic (knife or nailclipper), or stone (popular riot repressed in the blood). Unless, *simpliciter,* they are chunks of the Death-God Himself, decomposing waste smelling of thickened, nutrient grease. God as pudding.

2) The second kind of goodbye now up for discussion is of a subtler nature, hence it must be described and examined with loving, philological attention. We shall call this kind of goodbye "intrinsic". It's totally interior, internal, intimate: no need of external interlocutors, no question of being conditioned by external interference. It would not be rash, then, to affirm that due to the singular and exemplary purity of this style of goodbye, every other kind would like to join the family and take its place as low on the scale as the differtial requires, a unit of measure for all personal abrogation, a queen bee generating each miniscule larvum of renunciation.

This present study will, with didactic pertinacity, illuminate, as mentioned above, the necessary rather than the contingent quality of goodbye. Such a goodbye isn't made, isn't something that can be made nor sought to be made. It simply happens, such that in this instance there even ought to exist a moment in which it hadn't happened and thus its categorical quality would be invalidated. It's only through its own free compulsion to incarnate itself that it can dub words, gestures, and shadows by means of which it dresses its nonbeing in the wily clothes of being, which in itself is the essence, condition, and skeleton of being.

The intrinsic goodbye occurs solely and entirely in the *I*. By this I mean that which, under any name, agglomerates (with mixed, unreconciled feelings) around our expectation of death.

(Agglomerates around: we curl ourselves around death, nourishing ourselves from it through osmosis: you hear the soul's rumbling, its flatulence, the nighttime gurgling, the preverbal stench that already seems to bear witness to the digestion that's begun: then, deeper inside, fetuses glow phosphorescently among the ichthyic slime and minerals, nearly dead from growing through the long pregnancy, awaiting the good midwife who, by shattering that other body, will bring this body vital into life.)

From this point of view, then, the *I* is a place, a *hic;* thus we're wed to it at the *station,* or at the *funeral.* A transcendental place, metaphysical sign of the nail, or something less, the cleverness of direct address (like saying *Ladies and Gentlemen*) or of non-sense, seat of delirium, easy-chair of *dementia,* throne of stammering, bier of tingling nerve-ends. For we need a place where our goodbye can strut like an aging tenor; a backdrop, then, and stage-wings consecrated in a sonorous and fictive name by a stage direction devised *ab aeterno.* Discontinuous and imperilled, the *I* holds itself together by anagraphic alterations, trick photography, lap dissolves, special effects, a grating sound-track, a mending needle used as a seismograph, a poster with *Go To Lourdes* written on it, its opulent colors fading.

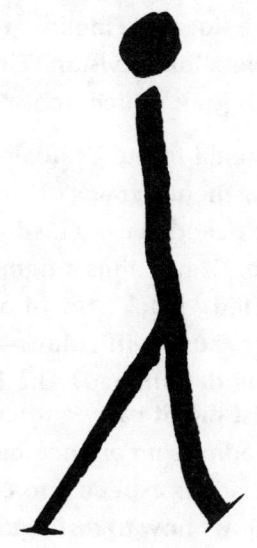

The Marginalist

EDWARD MARCOTTE

Where do I stand?—In the margin, looking along straight lines of text. The domain of the word—like rows of houses, streets of a city without end; rows of troops of some great army; rows of gravestones; rows of filing cabinets, archives of a mammoth enterprise. A universe I can observe only from outside: though I may traverse the space between lines I cannot enter the text. For that one must be a Textualist. Not having felt the Call, I remain a recalcitrant grey smudge in a world of black and white.

Not to say I'm a resister. Textualism, in its frantic dedication to the word, promulgates the slogan, "Fidelity to the Text." Deviation is punished by erasure, deletion, revision. The only real anomaly in a Textualist's universe is grey, which doesn't even exist.

The word "grey" is anathema to the Textualist. Grey-appearing is in reality a mosaic: homogeneous grains of either black or white—too fine, perhaps, for the naked eyes to distinguish, but easily observed with a microscope. Grey is thus a figment of our perverted senses, properly designated "black" up to a certain shade, and beyond that "white." This causes difficulties—which no one dares point out. How is the line determined? The institution of a standard, which any Textualist might carry and consult when needed would, apparently, be an admission of uncertainty concerning matters any right-thinking person is expected to catch at a glance. Nobody, as a result, really knows how to distinguish black from white.

Textualism harbors an even more ticklish paradox: as anyone may prove, a portion of those "pigmental atoms" are plainly grey, defying assimilation into black or white. The official argument out of this vicious circle rests on more powerful microscopes. Textualist engineers work frantically, devising even greater instruments of magnification, thus hoping to naturalize, once and for all, the grey fringe that nonetheless persists at each receeding level.

Infinitely patient, the Textualists. No one urging me to embrace the Truth. All the more oppressive: confidence inspires patience: truth, being universal, must ultimately reach the hearts of every last infidel. The maxim, "The Text will out," speaks for itself.

"Your statements are neither true nor false, but meaningless!" I want to cry. But such an outburst would meet only embarrassed silence.

Theoretically the norms and their enforcers are ideologically neutral. Coptors wear a white suit, pack a revolver, nightstick, stethoscope, and small flashlight, and are properly addressed as "Reverend." They have powers to detain, arrest, examine, club, perform minor revisions, officiate at funerals, weddings, and even baptisms. The regular coptor on the street, or the coptors in the various corrector-stations are supposed to enforce grammar without regard for rhetoric. Yet what's the difference? The temptation is great to confuse rhetoric with intelligibility itself. Hardly one in a million coptors aren't Textualists; moreover, all the schooling and exams taken by student coptors bear heavily on the Textualist style sheet. What more is there to say?

Textualism, by its pervasiveness, approaches invisibility. Overt deviation is rare enough to be equated with insanity. (The number of closet or latent deviationists is anybody's guess.)

My self-censorship faculties are tiptop: uttered "grey" but three times in all my months at the Temple. What happens in such cases? What happens to a Textualist? What happens if you let a fart in church? Nothing, in all three cases.

The world is one huge grey embarrassment: pavements, buildings, faces, the sky most of the time. Feel bloated with all those suppressed greys, ready to explode and bury everything in one great hot, sticky grey accident.

Despite the lack of rigorous objective criteria, appearances are carefully maintained, black-white mishaps rare. The marginalist is both defined and exposed by his proneness to such mishaps, his ostracism resting on nothing beyond this. Thus the Textualist may not even be distinguished by greater confidence: very likely we all harbor *equal* uncertainties in our hearts, every man a secret marginalist.

Throw the Book away, tear it up, burn it—you will find that books are the most indestructible of objects. Even if all copies of the Book are destroyed, does this mean that the Text no longer exists?

The Text is part of the Book but they are not the same. The Book remains unwritten. Text and margins have a parallel history, thus a contemporaneous end. Then what? Speculations vary. Some have suggested the heresy of a final merging of Text and margins. Undifferentiated grey, in other words. Hardly acceptable.

Only in the perspective of the Book is my existence recognized. You are holding the Book in your hands. Therefore you feel impervious, as though it were sufficient containment for the Text. But containers are subject to overflowing, perpetuating the challenge of the unaccountable. The snake, in swallowing itself, seeks to occupy the exterior margins of its existence, thus becoming its own double.

Conversations With the Minotaur

*on a plane somewhere between
psychodrama and guerilla theater*

BEV JAFEK

I. the minotaur's adolescence

I do not wish to be here I revile being here I am not-not here, my mother said to me.

Don't worry, I said, I'm certain you aren't, but even if you were, no one would believe you, so you are safe, nonetheless. A safe-secret.

That is all I am after, she said, *safe-secrets, you always put it so well though I despise having you about. You are obtrusively here, all the time. You are worse than a raw, open oyster. And covered with hair!*

It doesn't grow back in, you know.

Not that you would do anything about it if it did, she said.

It's true, I wouldn't. I would allow the entire cycle to unfold. The unimaginable, the imaginable, the reality. Hairy-outside, hairy-inside, defunct. And perhaps I would tickle myself to death perhaps in front of you. But you may find uncontrollable laughter to be quite unsettling.

You do everything in front of me. And everyone else, as well. Haven't I always tried to tell you that people who live in glass houses, if they must, shouldn't throw stones? And then go naked, jump insanely upon their bedsprings, and hoot, all with the lights burning like beacons and finally lock themselves out? You are not box-trained. And now I suppose it is too late.

One of the few advantages to the life of a beast is that she is no longer required to wear clothing. The glass house was not of my choosing. It has always existed alongside of my monstrous qualities, a blood-mother. Glass houses are not for the ordinary. And then my hooting—when one wishes to be understood, she speaks. When one wishes to devastate the sunny-vapid day of everyone else, she hoots. Glass houses and great hoots are a particularly appealing combination for me. As to the lassitude of our lives, we are frequently so. And when you find you are too late for yourself, it is imperative that you catch up as best you can and then run off in a completely different direction.

If I thought you really would do it, if I thought different directions existed and one could step upon them and not find them circular, leading one back to the start or somewhere very peculiar. I can't bear oddity. Perhaps you understand me though you are so extremely peculiar. I become confused when you say things like that to me, for they are full of hope, and hope is surely odd. I think to myself perhaps my daughter will go off and do some sort of new thing I have lost hope for the old ones and perhaps even a quiet one, that is not disgraceful. And truly not raucous. You have always been so raucous. Can you, really, go and do something that is not completely embarrassing to think of and quiet, as well?

The choice of direction is only the one that feels well beneath the feet.

Surely you will not run off without your shoes.

I may even leave my derby and necktie behind, but such is not nudity. It is a dismemberment prior to nudity.

And I have not felt the surface of my own skin. I must caress myself.

Sometimes the way you sound is still more bizarre than the way you look. All I understand is that when I look out to your glass house, there you are with your hooves, fangs, and nostrils pressed upon the window and blowing you are still blowing why are you always blowing that steam. Anyone at all who looks out sees a terrible cloud of gas with four odd little round objects there at the bottom and then your head, which is hideous enough without appearing to be squashed like a mound of cheese. It is pitiful the way the sky always shines so beautifully through the barren windows; the trees are visible in the forest beyond, one would say there is a wealthy, rustic hermit, perhaps delightful, who visits her mother once a year and is entirely charming, full of little gifts, and then you are there at the bottom all leveled out and distorted and full of overheated air. And the sounds that you make and that hooting, it makes no sense at all and is so disturbing. That such a thing should be allowed to live beside us when we go so well about our lives solving each little difficulty as we go so that nothing large and untidy will ever plop itself upon us and then there is this animal on a hill who just goes and toots out every bit of it. You are an unsolicited jack-o-lantern placed on my doorstep at Christmas. Can one not sit in a soft-silent place without these monsters of angles and twists loping up to disturb one? How much better I love my round sofas and soft lights!

I feel certain that I come from, if not a completely sympathetic and understandable line of thought, then what one might call a select, pneumatic few. Hilltops are, afterall, not unpopulated. There are earthworms, vegetables, toads, and occasionally an old beastwoman who bays, loud and unmercifully, at the moon and other objects of solitude, causing strange interventions to the earth's system of ear-and-eye, like media static and mythological fallout. Though they live beneath skies and furs, these animals have never complained of coldfeet. There are many more who believe they see the world through a pane of glass, but I will not mention them since there are so few hooters among them, and my pneumatic few must hoot at least for recreation. But above all else, there must be a grand old sense to the word *smut* which means the attempt, at one fine point of time, to do and say everything one is admonished not to, a kind of absolute whoring which, if whores had done, would have led to the disappearance of cities, of countries, and perhaps whole continents, and their replacement with harlotries, even a Union of Harlot States, in which I would, perhaps, have earned a small monthly income as a harlot subpotentate and if there is truth in this, I have a cultural origin, a tradition.

When someone, and particularly if it is really an animal, exceeds the bounds by a certain excess, it causes the audience to become squeamish. We can't listen and still maintain ourselves. And how can anyone be expected to think when they are squeamish!

Why don't you try screaming, instead?

I have tried everything I am capable of thinking upon, but I am beset by the strangeness of solutions. When they refuse to work for so long, I forget what they were intended for and I simply go on, solving and solving.

A maze of solutions! A formless thing filled with helium floating upon the air! Complete impotence and a red red balloon to show for it.

You know, one of the things I am most, most uncomfortable with in you is that when you best understand me, you are inscrutable. And I do not know how these two can be, one with the other.

It is a bizarre moment, trying to speak to one another over this distance. The cord was broken long ago. We share no food, the way friends do. And, of course, I cannot simply offer you some.

Why is that?

You are a cannibal.

I eat nothing but my living room these days.

That's true. You have been an arachnid for years now. It must be very painful.

It is so. As I look out, there is nothing that is out of place. I can wolf it all. Except for you. A monster is untouchable. Can you go live in the garden with the bulbs? I tried to eat them the other day, and they were indigestable.

Do you think I belong there?

You belong nowhere. But I thought there might be another indigestible thing out there, and you could make a fresh start with it.

Is there anything you want to know about me?

No, but since you will not leave, are you a member of the raucous parties or the several loud liberations or the quiet masses or the odd minorities or any of those?

I am not. Solely the barefoot minority.
Nearly decent. Hobbies?
None. Slowly I have become entirely serious.
What do you do in your spare time which, by the looks of things, is perpetual?

My own perpetual time. An intransigent space, for my thoughts are the sole occupant. In spite of yourself, as you so often are, you ask about the glass house where I lie pensively upon my tail, peering and steaming. Now I see that you are curling over yourself like a banana, and from this strange activity, I infer you are falling asleep on me, which has never failed to incite me toward answering your questions. My first point will be, then, that I hate glass. I would much prefer cork, even wood for my house or dense paper, perhaps the last veins of silver, aluminum at the least. But glass is illusion disembodied. Imagine a whore made of glass and perhaps you will feel the mystery. How simply, it seems, you are part of the surface beyond it, how easily you could take a great roll upon your belly and be a terrible hairy pleasureboat all the way, down the hill or not; but so close to it that some things would be shared, like air, and the separation would make no difference, at least not while the wind blows. But one hoof, one curious snout, one small fang-print through it, and the storm explodes upon you, of crystal and pain, and then the exquisiteness, the terrible yearning, just before and just after. And the mirrors, revolving, to the walls to all the wheedling paradoxes. Of a mystery, there is a twining together of things; a twist of center and its circumlocution, this bending toward, at one time. So of our glass mirrors, for the bounds of them, for the image of traveling both into, and out of, them and, the strangeness; remaining onething. Bleep-bleep. Bleep-bleep. The computer is speaking to you. You have now utilized your daily allotment of evasiveness, and you must awaken and become sober and miserable. It is the computer's dearest wish. Bleep-bleep. Awaken, dear mother. Bleep-bleep. Bleep-bleep.

You are making animal sounds again! Stop those animal cries!

They are not animal cries. Bleep-bleep. Bleep-bleep. They are the sounds of a machine, the great computer.

Stop it! Stop it! All I do is go to sleep and you go mad in the interim.

I have decided to give up hooting forever. I will now solely bleep. Bleep-bleep.

Now I must listen to this when I was so soundly asleep and then I had a dream and now I am here with you again and you are more hideous than ever.

Tell the computer your dream.

I cannot tell you! It was very personal and besides, you will do something bizarre if you hear of it.

I will do something bizarre anyway. Tell the computer your dream, or she will go on bleeping.

Will you really stop?

The computer is incapable of untruth.

Well I dreamt that you were Christ.

Perhaps that will be next on the computer's list of masturbatory entertainments.

No, I mean that you really were.

Well, there is nothing real here, so that must be excluded. Tell the computer the details of your dream.

Everyone said that you were divine, and that was why you were so ugly.

Perceptive, divinities are distinctly funny-looking. Perhaps because they reflect their creators.

Tell me, again, how it is that you make sense?

If they tell you you're a strange one, you've not heard anything until you get up to the mirror yourself.

Are you making an oblique criticism of mirrors?

Which one? I'm talking about the one that reflects thoughts, the annoying one.

Well back to my dream.

I assume.

And so I said to myself, if it's only that she's divine, then I suppose it's not so awful.

Your suffering justified.

Then they crucified you.

My suffering unjustified. Was it the usual—blood and so forth?

It was just terrible. But it was also inspiring and beautiful.

Blood always is.

Then you died and they threw you away.

Am I not supposed to have an expensive crypt?

Yes then they took you back, or someone did, and put you in a crypt.

Thank god for propriety. And did I not rise from the dead?

After a few days, they all heard you hooting in there and then some steam blew out.

I had come to my senses, in other words.

Yes unfortunately, you were just as you always are.

Just as I was; then divinity, now minotaur, what did I do and then what did they do about it to protect themselves?

You were supposed to push aside the stone that covered the crypt you know you were supposed to do it! It was so annoying.

You mean that I didn't? I, a divinity, the savior of humanity?

No you didn't. You just hooted and steamed in there, and we knew you were Christ but you couldn't get back out again. I have never been so ashamed of you.

Now that is considerable. But then, dreams accentuate things. I would defend myself by saying that this did not, in reality, happen; but I suppose that makes no sense to you.

Nothing you do ever does. I cried in to you and I said, if you would just do some exercises, some push and pull-ups and not spend all of your time hooting and steaming and sitting on your tail, then you could come out and be Christ and everyone would admire you. They would forget your ugliness, and you would not have to feel sorry for yourself.

And, of course, you could be the Virgin Mary.

Yes and I could be her. Perhaps she wouldn't mind.

Fascinating, rambunctiously fascinating. The virgin who gives birth to the female Christ is entirely free of her keeper. A congenial transformation of the myth, a causing to self-copulate, a triumph, and my mother is a divine thief beneath it all. Remove your floppy hat, dear mother, perhaps you have the rudiments of horns!

Something odd has happened again.

It always does. The mirror, the room of glass.

That was the other odd thing I didn't quite grasp. May I get back to my dream?

Inevitable.

I called and called in to you, but it did no good at all.

And absolutely nothing from me? Did I not utter any words of remorse? Was my despair not apparent to everyone and above all else, did no one come to shut me up?

I read you the entirety of an exercise book. And then I started on a self-assistance manual.

And I grew more and more still with lacerating boredom until I really did perish.

The steam did go down to the trickle of a cigar.

You really have created a tragedy—murder through self-assistance. That's worth a few puffs, if you'll pardon me. Anyway, a frustration-dream, it must have been. They say we have them all the time. When we are frustrated. And dreaming. At the same time. A frustration dream—that explains it.

It explains nothing! You could have been Christ, and you hooted it all away.

Before you become compulsive about Mary and Christ, I think you should know that a *man* came to the door while you were snoring away.

He did! What did he do and say? Did you scare him away?

Not exactly. That does not define, with precision, our transaction. He said, I have heard from mysterious sources that you are a divinity, and the word has passed through our tiny village. Thus I am here as quick as a lump to collect your autograph and a pinch on your twat, babes.

My word! It had passed through his tiny village and he called you babes?
As befits a divinity.
Perhaps it is all true; everything that I dreamed.
Yes, it may be. But then, of course, I had to answer him.
Oh you didn't start hooting, did you?
I never start. I have always hooted and always will. I said kind sir who calls me babes, there's no one here but us minotaurs. No divinities, nope, none nowhere. But since you've made this long pilgrimmage, I'll just give you my autograph anyway. Then I stuck my hoof onto his ink-pad and laid him a good one in the stomach.
You struck him I have no desire to hear anything from you again but what did he do?
He screamed. And then he ran all the way down the hill.
You could have made them think you were divine. They are such fools they will believe anything and here you told them you were a monster.
I am compulsively truthful. A terrible habit.
You could have made them believe anything, and you just stuck out your damned hoof.
I'm probably spastic, too. No control over the tonus.
You are not really a minotaur! You are a mildly feral young woman who could benefit from a bit of electrolysis and plastic surgery.
That's a minotaur. And you can pull a beast to the electrocutioner, but you can't make her self-amputate.
Perhaps I shall never sleep again.
Think of all you could accomplish.

I have never known a thing so indigent as an indigent female deviant.

Just like the fact that there is nothing so pregnant as a pregnant cat. Naively one believes that there are certain absolutes in this world—pregnancy, indigence, humanity, divinity—and then one finds that it is completely false; for some are men, some are women, after all, just like us, after all.

It amounts to nothing and here I screamed and screamed and wailed to you, I don't know for how long but it was so very long and oh, how you waste time above all else.

Of course I waste time—I am at the end of history. What is ongoing, now, cannot continue to do so. There is no better purpose for my fangs than to chomp it. Beyond my pane of glass, the livable assumption is that it is not here, ongoing, because no one can see it clearly, swinging its finger like a traffic policeman. But perhaps the tactile approach is better, the grasp by the neck's nape, like meets like. Then you try chomping away at it, and there is indeed a thick strip of bloody meat below your fangs. You gag up to your snout. We are all turning into monsters for it, and there are no more dentists to save us.

I remember when you were a little girl, and you were not hideous then. A lovely little thing, you were, a sylph. Those fangs were the first to come in. They were such baby buds at first, almost beautiful, and I thought what a strange little creature I have made, I nearly love her this way and so I will play with her for a bit. For just a tiny rolling nugget of time, and then I will murder her. She will grow into a fine young rectangle like the others. But for now, I thought, I was never allowed to play with strange little things, not matches, not tiny knives on a chain, not even a dog. And so I said it is alright, then, I can play with this little mystery, and she will live for a bit. No one will ever see these tiny buds growing in her mouth. I will decorate them with rings, tie bows on them, and make her beautiful. A baby minotaur has such huge, silent eyes. It is a baby-bundle of mood. Any mother who could keep one hidden away would do it. And so I let you live, on and on, and I let time roll away with you. There are few who would brave it, though. One can be murdered by the bedtime-ape for keeping such a thing. He must never see you, as we were, playing by ourselves, and I always let you laugh until your little budded fangs hung out. I remember how he would drool when he saw you. How his eyes would bulge. It gave me strange shivers how it made me feel very strange. I loved making him drool and letting you keep your little budded fangs. I thought what a terrible imp of a mother I am what little gusts of pink terror I cause here what a fumarole and so delicate I am, if you can make them, those tiny buds and that pale stream of drool and still stay so very slight in spite of it, then they will all feel like monsters, all the bedtime-apes, how they will roll in front of you for the slightest chance to make human sound again, and only, so secretly, to you, how they will softly, silently, and in such little gusts, despise themselves, and perhaps I can murder then yet how I will sing and dance and be so very delicate when I sink the knife oh a knife for me, a little one a pink one covered with ribbons and bows. I am a dancer, a singer, where most mothers would let you suffocate in the cookie-jar. They would ram your baby-toothbrush down your little throat. I am different. I am, really, to myself, very very odd. I cannot bear anything at all. I would love to play and play with strange little things, sing and dance, and then go into the cookie jar myself.

I have the strangest sensation of having heard this all before. Do you suppose that you tell me this story everyday, and then I forget it, everyday, except for my irritation? That would make sense—we are an ongoing, flexible sea of irritation. One should consider all the alternatives, particularly when one feels foolish.

And I remember when you began to grow up oh time is so delicate then. It can burst in all directions. It is a mother more terrible than I, for it can punish everything; and slowly, quietly, with intricate patterns, almost beautiful. One must duck from it, then, and one must kill a baby minotaur when she is very young. When she has grown a bit, even the fire department cannot save you. I remember how you would defy us all to live. I would no more than place a grocery sack on the floor than you would charge it with your tiny horns. How you practiced destruction like a piano lesson. And how could I refuse you, I hid you in the attic, instead, I hid you in the basement, your little hooves waved in the air above the breadbin, you steamed from the toilet bowl like a small geyser and our home was very, very odd. The bedtime-ape lived on, bulging and drooling until, one day, he did not. And you put your little hooves around my waist and said mama, mama, give me a cooked lamb! Which beast, I would hum, gaily then and to myself, should I serve and then what laughter shall I have when I am all alone and rid of them all. Let them charge one another, then, and let them starve with their horns lodged in the wall. I will murder nothing but this tiny space, this delicate land, about me.

Has your tongue turned black recently?

I believe I once saw a black pit at the center of my face. Do you want to look?

Yes I am quite fascinated.

It will wobble.

No matter. There are times when you seem complex.

Well, you see this pit is quite simple. It is no more than a hole, really. There is simply nothing there, one might say, at a certain spot; specifically my mouth.

But it is very curious that I should find this objectlessness in you when I have never noticed it before and, furthermore, you are generally as simple as a lump of butter.

I find it somewhat bizarre myself; however, not beyond the bounds, that is, not beyond what is vaguely absent of atrocity. That is one thing I have kept to myself in the midst of all this ruckus—vague absence of atrocity.

I thought I would just look in, if I may.

Oh please do. Feel quite free.

Real expanse ongoing there. One senses great distances. And absolutely nothing. It is just as you say—pure vacancy.

I have always felt that I described my condition quite well, and I will always do so, with nonchalance or mild drama, whatever is necessary, and whenever anyone appears interested. That is how one gets through these little things.

But my curiosity.

Oh please be curious. I am not concerned in the least. I could have had two broken legs instead, but this was my choice. And now I refer to it, often fondly, as my specialty.

Do you ever swallow wind?
Wine?
No, wind.
Whine?
Wind.
Oh, wind. Yes, well, often, but that is not the worst of it. That is hardly anything at all. I have to be quite careful of my surroundings, watch them with great caution, sometimes spray fumigant all over myself at certain intervals because I accidently fall asleep quite easily, a small weakness, and there are things that can crawl in there.
All the way in, they crawl?
Yes, they do. Sometimes I positively bulge for them. And don't imagine that they are proper. I wobble totally then. Really, there is no treatment for it but to spray regularly.
Then do you feel at all naked? I mean that there is some part of yourself that all may see, irrespective of whom, and anytime, whether you wish it or not; though, in your case, there is absolutely nothing there?
Oh never that, never, really, I would despise it and furthermore, I would feel so globular.
Globular?
Yes. Globular.
Oh.
Yes?
I have a feeling this has come to an end.
Not at all. I am perfectly willing to discuss my condition with anyone, even the rankest of animals, so you see I am quite reasonable. I even apologize. Would you like to hear an apology?

In absence of all else, like the center of your face, alright.

Well, there are things that happen most very small, most inconsequential, and so it makes no difference if we are a bit strange from time to time, and in little bits. We say, and as quietly as possible, avert your gaze slightly, you may still look at me side-long and I at you, we may gaze and gaze, though side-long, please do not look too closely at my little hole and then I will not listen so carefully to your gelatinous speech. Now does that not make fine sense? We compromise, just a bit, and then we may sit and gaze side-long to our heart's content. If you would simply learn to live in little bits, and gaze side-long, you would not be absolutely horrible, as you are.

I believe this has become something other than an apology. But, of course, that is only one beast's opinion.

Now that was well-done. A compromise. You're doing it, at last. The opinion of one and, of course, there are many.

But so few monsters.

And that was well-thought. You make up such a tiny group, after all, though you are so large yourselves. You will note I said "large" rather than "over-sized." I compromise, if only given the chance. Now I will turn my head from you ever-so-slightly.

I see you, nearly, halved. Subtle.

Again so. And you may compliment me occasionally, as well.

Can you turn your head even more?

Of course. Now I am staring at the kitchen wall.

Is it striking? Does it fascinate you?

I make no criticism of it. It is mine, after all.

Then just remain like that. It will be pleasant.
Do you think so? Do you concern yourself with my feelings as I look off?
Yes and my own, as well.
Then perhaps we can get along.
Perhaps so.
I find my walls to be so very kind. Perhaps you find it odd to call a wall kind, but it is really all that is kind. Now I feel like telling you all the little strange things, I don't know why. Perhaps it is because I cannot see you. Your ugliness is so distracting. I don't see how anyone can speak with you; but then, perhaps they don't. Perhaps you are rarely concerned. They say some animals are made of rubber, like cats. Perhaps you are like a cat. I have come to feel affection for these little walls, do you know? I am a mother, at heart, and they are my good-daughters. I have 29 of them, my 29 daughters. Sometimes they breathe, just a bit. Oh it's true, you can see them moving at night. You can touch them, and they are such warm happy-good flesh. I am so comfortable with them, so pleasantly pleased. There are no angles in this room if my little walls are flesh. There is just a continuation of a body which was once my own. How comforting it is to think of it going on and on and never stopping, to everywhere at once, and it is quiet, believe me, it is not as raucous as the world. We would be better for it. I am no opportunist for wishing these things, I am a reformer, and furthermore, you cannot throw me in jail for it because I only think it at three o'clock in the morning. That is, of course, when I nibble my livingroom to pieces.

I have heard you at that. I don't call myself a moralist, but it is one of the most terrible sounds I have ever heard.

That is the only little noise I make, my late-at-night gnaw. How I have shoveled and shoveled away. I have bitten and clawed at them, all of my angles. I have sawed them off. I have swallowed a light bulb and glowed for two hours. Have you wondered have you pondered where the sewing machine went when it went and the refrigerator and the tables and chairs, the banister, the stairs, I am the omnipotent stomach that polished them all off, I am the one, the deep-hole for a life. And then I lick and I lick.

Out with it. I see it now. I know about you.

Oh you do? Did you guess my little secret just now? Or before?

One might say that I guess everything and know nothing. But out with it. I have my curiosity.

Oh yes, your curiosity. I believe that is what began this when it began. Well, there is not only vacancy at the center of my face. There is also my coal-black tongue!

Yes, I can see it now. But out with it. It must be over two feet long.

Oh no, it is not so very odd. I would estimate that it is, only, ten inches, thus far. It may grow to a full two feet, but it is not that now, and unpredictable, of course.

You cannot let it hang out?

I have rarely let anyone see, it is so peculiar. They see it even if they gaze side-long. But perhaps I can let it hang if you will promise me to look side-long anyway.

My head is appropriately cocked.

Then here it is.

(Flop)

Your coal-black tongue is at least three feet. Perhaps four.

Ah, I had hoped it was not. But then, I stopped measuring it after the age of forty.

It has been growing, there, so long?

It has.

And you have kept it a secret; except, I suppose, when you ate spaghetti?

I have, except to other old women.

Others have them, too?

Yes, and it is such a comfort when we get together and let it all hang out. You have never been to an old womens' group meeting. No one ever does come but ourselves. So we are perfectly safe to lie on the floor with them all hanging out and that is just what we do.

And nothing more?

No, that is really the all of old womens' group meetings. We have centers all over the country where we lie on the floor and just let it all hang out. It is a wonderful secret, for no one pays us the slightest attention, and they will never know of our customs. Oh, it does feel so very nice to do it. Much better than it feels alone. Then you always get hungry and you lick and lick into all the corners of the room.

That is what I have heard. That soft, smacking sound late at night, like an eternal childrens' cereal.

It was I. I do not eat or sleep. I am perpetually busy at odd tasks and at night, late with my bones lit by the pallid light of an egg who eats its skin over and over again, an old fool whom all have left to starve. There was a time, oh eons ago, when I said I will not munch my little limbs from tip-to-toe (like this perverse old egg) in tiny bits swallowed from cookie-cutters. There is another thing to be and to rest in, for the world, at least, will have rest in it. I will be that which is like a tree by the oceanside, blown back, assiduously, till it arcs upon itself. I will be that which is never varnished which is porous which is permeated by all things, and they will sit upon me like a flock of birds. A great long skirt I will wear hiding lambs and doves, a mouse curled in my ear, a swallow on my finger for a ring, a lizard in my nose. Oh they will perch on me and hide in me and ravish me, for I will always be their scarecrow in the wind. I will dance my great dance headless and legless, the rooted one, the swollen torso with the vines and the children and all the clinging things. There I will be, blowing blowing and billowing with my million lovers. But the arc comes round and the vines and the fish and the wind recede, like gums in my old-woman's mouth and there is nothing left but an empty hole and all the cracking and creaking of an old woman. Then it is that I let my ancient black tongue crawl all over the room trying to pick-pick-pick at whatever might be. I hallucinate crumbs from time to time, and I nearly strangle on them, that is more peculiar than anything else. How I can nearly die for them, these things that are not there. Old women are beasts, too, they are monsters like everyone else but it is always for these things that are not there, these little bits for which we go pick-pick-pick and now you know it all, you hound, you blasphemer, my perfect devil-daughter. I would never have answered but for the fact that now, at this moment, you are not here, either, you are a crumb for which I go pick-pick-pick.

II. the minotaur in love

A tale has an edge, beyond which it does not extend. It may appear to close here, or even end; unless you are viewing the whole, in which case it does not. This bound is its reality, the angle of a crystal which touches another surface; the whole existing as a point where all angles occlude inward upon themselves. Such a closing, this last minister to a word-congregation, is the fact that Theseus killed the male minotaur. The female minotaur was so monstrous that he could not imagine her. But the imagining of the thing, the mind's flicker and indiscernable hum along its own current, is the sole means of approach, attack, or interact in this particular labyrinth, though there are others with different assumptions for being. In consequence, the female minotaur lives on in her labyrinth. She would have murdered herself long ago but for a fabled mishap: she met another minotaur, an equal monstrosity. Ah, my scuzzy-one, you are for me; I am a lesbian, what, pray, art thee? She said to the other minotaur and to be understood, but more, to make delicious her gaucheries. Not more nor all that is imputed and not intending to obfuscate, yet; at one time a man, but not, in resolution, then I was even more a woman, but misplaced, as can so often be so, and arighted, as it were, with the blessings of surgery but then, through this happening, which was also a labeling, transsexual yet not in my own mind no, merely in reality, at the bound, therefore and finally, a minotaur, like yourself. But take not truck with the strangeness of things, for our labyrinth breathes both in and out; the inspiration in what we will only say in the unreal center, the metaphor, all the while we expire in these shrinking and abrasive corridors where one thing meets with another. You are the strangest being I have seen in all of my twistings and twinings about; as such, lucid and beautiful, to me. If our four fangs will permit of a bit of nuzzling, I am ready for you, my minotaur-love. *The monsters touched, played with one another's shaggy manes, and finally embraced on bended hoof. They surmised that the course of love should lead them quickly to the most exquisite of pleasures, since their lives had previously been devoid of such considerations. Thus the desire to destroy came upon them. And as many a beast has bellowed out, there is a simplest and most wonderful vehicle for destruction—the things one calls a belongingness, those eyes who were never invited to the dance. The monsters built a great conflagration, threw in their possessions, and lay down beside it peering in pure wonder from beneath their great manes and caressing each other with their hungry hooves.*

Outside, the megalopolis grows and grows, but inside, here, where you touch the tale, we sit beside the oldest hearth of woman-kind. The orange light burns mysteriously in the eyes of the two beasts as they explore one another with their great, furry lips and intuit all that may be known of monstrosity. Together, we will make such monsters as the world has not seen since its beginning, *the minotaur whispers to her shaggy lover. And though they are lying still, there is something that rebounds from them, stirs, and gallops. One imagines it running endlessly in this labyrinth; which is, after all, as simple as a glass room, filled with nothing save what is imputed to it, the monsters who are always behind the blinds, an ideal space for the race of semantics. But such presumptions are untrue, for this is the monster that always exceeds the bounds, the recommended dosages. It is pure motion. It is the metaphor that disdains all others. I cannot give you a happy ending, my darling, my fanged one, says the minotaur, but I can give you a two-headed antelope of delight. It dances, now, beside our fire.*

The minotaur rolls back her huge, terrible head and dreams she has become a human being again.

We Only Want You To Be Happy Janet

SAMANTHA POMERANCE

We only want you to be happy Janet. Want you this fine December morning made of rain, of reservations, to be glad.

We are filling up rooms overlooking the park. Outside the old men of Christmas are marching. Holding their prescriptions in their hand they shake to Good King Wensceslaus, tremble to Silent Night.

We have torn up, removed the Birches from the ballroom. We have put in random planking, have constructed all the doors. Inside doors, screen doors, cellar doors, and the frigid French doors too. Preening, the early winter lamplight throws itself across our knees. We are thinking for a moment of the Bosphorous Straits. Of the fearless fishes flying. Of the silver New Year shadows.

Will they make it up to us for lunchtime? For Cleopatra? For the Royal Russian Children? "Yes, yes," we cry. We shake our curls like omens 'round our head. Laughing, the ardent cellar doors burst open.
Inside her icebox, waiting for the end, Mrs. O. O. Smith
sings radio-news songs.
"Checking and cross-checking and analyzing the results,"
she sings,
"we find
no profound shift from that position
in the day to day thinking of consumers
according to Bourgoine."

Over our polished ballroom floor, across the random planking, we watch in triplicate, our best regards, our winter conversations.

Tonight the ghosts are calling Catherine. Mrs. O. O. Smith, assembled in her white cocoon, smiles gently at the silken evening voices. "Catherine," they call her, "Catherine." And Catherine's hair, tied up in ringlets in the back, curls like the hair on the heads of pretty women. "And whose little girl are you?" they ask. And Catherine knows, and Catherine tells the answer.

A serious matter has been brought to our attention. We are reminded of the Causian Wars, the Celt and Arabic Invasions. The streets fill up with taxicabs, with ledger books, with Very truly yours.

Calling upon the correcting device, we find it sits in perfect working order. We wipe our shoes off on the mat, leave cards engraved and shining on the silver platter. We set the margins, roll our sleeves, correct the careless error. Completing our correction we observe, the streets fill up with carriages, with how-dee-doo's, with nice to know you.

Inside her icebox, having found the end, Mrs. O. O. Smith sits quieter than Tuesday morning. Her hair hangs down in licorice strings, in badger bones, in inconsiderations. If God had meant her to call Tuesday, he would have combed her Tuesday hair, have shined her Tuesday sandals.

Janet, we will dance again. Dance though our sons desert us, our legs ignore us, our arms have gone to rust. On point. This evening. At tonight's performance. Three hundred thirty-two fuétés. How they will shout for us, will cry for us, will throw us all their roses.

In the dark our Janet listens, smiles, adjusts her Easter skirts. We only want her to be happy.

The Woman Beautiful
A treatise by an eminent Victorian alchemist

OPAL L. NATIONS

.1.

Youth, health and beauty are the three qualities
sought by womankind, 'tis known that women seek
out the youth, thus attain him, and lavish upon
him all of her ugliness, so when the body is thus
attoned antiseptic spasms occur, like resplendent
tides of radio wave frequencies generated by the
now inert immobile self. Health absorbs beauty,
the pharmacy of passing time, a health itself fed
of beauty's own aura, the nectar, the sweet irre-
sistible thirst breaker, at first the wine that
flows through arterial goblets plentifully qualifies,
but as the insatiable body lusts for that last drop
of sensual visibility, ugliness is incurred and
youth is sought.

Perhaps in the triple quest beauty stands first,
the grease paint of the plastic surgeon, the distance between observance and reality, for it is
hard to think of beauty without roses, and roses
without thorns.

Keep healthy, and you will keep youth for as long
as the sum of the parts divides the space of
ethereal reality.

* * *

.2.

You can cheat Father time and hold him at bay,
moisten the tips of your fingers with saliva,
hold them outstretched in front of you in a dark
room of drawn blinds, think of the appearance of
a sharp crystal vigorously cutting through a
bloodstream of dying cells, inhabitants of a
world in the neuro-regions of the mind.

* * *

.3.

The first fault of the woman who is growing in
years is the figure, a perceptual ease, an electrical
device which generates thought, a sophistication of
preparatory access. It grows heavy and offensive
for beyond absolute perfection lies a charmless
theatre of disposed and divided truths, awkward
principles and a passing disintegration of still
remembered primordial essences, the clot of blood
in the eye of the sun.

THE WOMAN BEAUTIFUL

.4.

The woman becomes a middle-aged figure, the generations
of accident are seeping into her, she sleeps a little
longer in the morning for when she sleeps the ancestral
change of appearance, the evolution of perfect attain-
ment flows through the body like an embalmer's fluid.

* * *

.5.

The figure is a little more tired during the day,
some atoms in the composite of things escape her
view, the world is losing form by a gradual process, brought about partly by the altering spaces,
which by now lose personal symphony, withdrawing
away to places where the human being is a little
less mature.

* * *

.6.

The middle-aged figure will eat more, her ancestors
have a hold on her, they pull furiously at the outer
skin, wrinkles occur, earth spirits start parting
weeds and grass, a spiritual body-print is made for
the interment of the body to be.

* * *

.7.

She also goes to bed earlier, they call her when
creeping like pores of perspiration over her abdomen,
beckoning her to go with them into the night where
a family of apes and monkeys, and even amphibians
are waiting to draw from her her part of painful
existence, they need her, she is invaluable to them,
for the sight of paradise requires that she gives
one of her eyes for all of them, the unattainable
is once again in mind, until her children fasten
themselves to the endless embroidery.

Women, Like Horses

DICK HIGGINS

English as it is spokgen. Spogken? Englio. Ao it io opokgen. In Brooklyn & by Emelie.

Emelie. The flower. La francesca. But very much of De Kalb Avenue. Once who working where I was working. Having been there for ages before me. So long. Many years before having brought roller skates to work. Skating the length of the printing plant during lunch hour, back and forth. Swooping like a high up crane, past the Big Chief presses and the Davidsons. Never being old, being always young. A plant, a structure. But not to balance. To balance only on your skates and on your life.

Yvonne very different. Harnessing her troops. Men, women, all the same. Group of five going together here. Group of eight going together there. Seeming to ignore the audience. But never going offstage. Ignoring the audience, huh? But why not going off the stage? People going together. No women, no men, only bearers of certain plumbing.

Emelie on skates. Working. Not working. Telling about her brother dying of cancer. So many air purifiers having to be there. Her brother so horribly embarrassed. To smell. To stink repulsively. A delicate man dying, and smelling like a bad joke. As dying, being. Only thirty five. And knowing one really is making poisonous air.

Yvonne, reading from Lennie Bruce. Telling about saying something very dirty: snot. Telling about snot and disgust. Snot being a natural excretion from certain membranes. With a connotation of illness and therefore revulsion. And an ability to ruin suede leather. Or velvet or velveteen no doubt. Snot? Snot being something cleaned up, usually.

And Emelie. Fond of Chinese food. And fond of my then assistant—now known as a very good artist, though also as a dealer in blue and white pills—but never much good at making and designing bank checks at Emelie's company. That being what we were doing and which for whatever perverse or twinkly reasons, some of us muchly enjoying doing. Emelie on the phone. On the phone? With whom? With Elvis Presley, doing some checks for Gladdys Music, that being his mother's name and the name of a music company in her name. Those checks having a particularly good picture of Elvis Presley on them. Elvis happy. Elvis on the telephone with Emelie.

Yvonne's group, one moving like the next. One calling out "reverse" when they get near the wings. Or moving as two groups of threes. If three sexes, three groups? The threes leading and following. Ciphers on an empty blackboard. Not really moving so much as proposing and disposing. Like an accountant of motion.

And Mildred running the printing press. Imprinting the bank checks with magnetic ink. A then-new machine, the A. B. Dick #1700, very accurate, very fast. Black Mildred, a militant in those far off early 60's days. Mildred festive in a green dress in the office at Christmas party time. The boss having left after a swift toast. Wild? No, but festive. Mildred saying, "I'm for the em-ploy-yees, not the boss." So different from Mary, Queen of the Collating Line, racing and assembling multiple part invoices, never known to speak. Or Peanuts. Later Peanuts gone to the place where sweet folk go who develop occupational allergy. Anything Peanuts not allergic to? Poor Peanuts. But Mildred crackling and sparkling. Having a daughter—"don't ask me where she came from,"—and glittering in her green dress or her uniform. Overcoming so many things. And grinding the work out and living her life with a snip of glee.

During the snot reading, a film on the screen. A naked man.

A naked woman. A genteel apartment. A huge balloon. The balloon tossed back and forth. No sex. Just tits bobbing. Balls bobbing. No smiles on faces. Just shifting of seats. Passing the balloon. Man on the seat, balloon to his right. Woman sitting to his right. Removing balloon. To man's left. Man going to other side of balloon. All that plumbing. Moving around. Man occasionally smirking. Slightly. Cool. Woman removing balloon. Replacing it. Cold. All that plumbing. Woman smiling. Film ending.

Other women. Other jobs. My first boss, a woman. In a Public Relations firm. So liberal! Not a work think looked back at happily. Becoming a good researcher, under Miss Victory. Not happy for a writer, recalling that his first published work being a history of the eating of roast beef in the English-speaking world. For a roast-beef selling company. Poor Miss Victory, conquering the land of meat-eaters, selling beef. Ann Victory, poor Ann. Stout and thirties-ish. A spiritual tenant of the meat eaters. And the building owned by a federation of something ostensibly Jewish. But no good Jewish food being sold there. Having to go out far to get a good pastrami. A place with many serious people. Talking about would they do Public Relations for a communist regime? Many days spent discussing would they support the Columbian revolution. Letting alone Cuba. Ann Victory, looking for goodies in the newspaper morgues. I, finding a useful corpse, a mention of 6/12 lotion in some encyclopedia. 6/12 being a client. Ann being so excited. Doing the right things to bring this to the public's attention. And laughing with me over the whole thing.

Yvonne at an earlier dance. Cool. Tossing with red balls like a child. So fresh. The group of people not so rigid. Suddenly Bach's "Schlummert ein" from the "Ich habe genug" cantata. Yvonne: "I love you." He: "I love you." Yvonne: "I've always loved you." He: "I've always loved you." Yvonne: "I've never loved you." He: "I've never loved you." Electricity, and perhaps a little tragedy. Playing with the balls.

Seeing Ann later. Suddenly so different. Married first and pregnant then. I, looking for work just then, coming by and seeing her. Seeing her happy. Ann laughing at years of publicity work, throwing a child in their faces. A forbidden and tasteless thing in a time without children. Without children?—bloody virgins. Running away from the role role.

Other ways of doing it? Yvonne? Perhaps. Beautiful, a thing just about as it is. Beautiful? Not a thing as it is but a thing about it. An isolated thing. A harmony or an empathy with something about something. Things being about things.

A dream. From Chuang Tzü. Horses having hooves. To walk in the grass with. Long ears to hear with. Noses for smelling leaves. Eyes for telling when the sky is bluest. Horses. Horses among the bushes. Horses nuzzling the junipers. Horses without saddles. Horses laughing in the mist. Horses eating grain. Horses and wet hay. Horses gobbling oats. Horses drunk on eating fallen apples. Horses in the morning. And in the evening. The night the horses ran loose, and the long-haired girls, fifteen or so, my daughters perhaps, running after them. Sartje and Charity, Hannah and Jessie. In front of the charge, Zinez, an albino donkey, ghostly in the dark. Out from the barn—unlatched by Zinez, past the pig pen. Past the little bridge over the creek, up the hill, past the maple sugar house. Into the woods.

This not about women but men and women. To saddle a horse or a girl or a boy. Just more obvious about some. Obvious; as one being obvious. Fat men, oozing in bulbous girdles, weighted down by bulbous testicles in every thinking, feeling, speaking. Women simply cramped on principle.

The problem never Yvonne or Emelie, Mildred or Ann, Frank or Bill or John or Ralph. But to be tender and particular. A being, the smallest of things. An individual louse or god, somewhat better.

Other things coming later. Men being like horses too.

I Had Never Noticed

CHARLIE SISE

I had never noticed until tonight how vicious the wind gets in February on the corner of Bleury and Sherbrooke. Maybe my coat is unbuttoned, but my hands are in my pockets and they're not fixing to move. I'm just not ready to play ball any more with the local demons who say, "Ho! Ho! Lend us your fingers for a while, darling, and we'll relinquish your guts and genitals."

My guts and genitals have stood worse in their uneventful lives and they can take it—but why do they have to?

I wonder what colours they are wearing tonight. My balls remain sweetly mysterious, they have cowered back into their prenatal haunts now, but I like to think of them glittering there foggily like those marbles with clouds under their skins. My cock beeps faintly under white crusts of rime like tiny Radium under Ungava. And coming around to my guts I know it's tough to think of them being the colour of aluminum or steel, but it would be too laborious a lie to dig up a more genial shade for them.

I've heard our intestines are coiled so intricately that if anyone had the heart to unwind them, he would be amazed at their length. Mine are stretched out straight and steel now, like the tram-rails humming in the wind down the centre of Sherbrooke St., for miles the only visible source of sound—and if you want to know how long they've become, don't even think of asking me; ask the rails how long the wind is.

Strange that nobody's removed them, those rails. I don't know how long ago the last streetcar sailed down them, to end up a hot-dog stand shorn of wheels on a lonely country road, but it was probably before I learned to count anyway and I don't remember when that was. Besides, Miss Stark, I'm still shaky on all units between seconds and centuries.

A friend (not a friend. He tried to make out I was worse off than him and I wasn't sure whether to believe him) a friend of mine harbours an immense nostalgia for those streetcars. On warm Sundays he tours the museum pieces at the old MTC tramyards for hours, smiling and crying.

I told him once: "It doesn't matter. The streetcars ran on rails of frustration."

"So what?" he said—or am I making this up now? "The buses run on wheels of frustration." Now, please, God, tell me if I'm personalizing. I don't want to be caught out here personalizing with no one around.

This silence is unbearable. A car went by here a minute ago making no noise at all, and I know it's not just the snow that muffles everything, I know it's not just the night that gets between me and the buildings and the barber's three-flavoured pole, the traffic lights, and the frozen Christmas stars, till their shimmer grows thin and I try to remember what dream they occurred in long ago.

All things recede, even your lover's most unexpected smiles, say the dying, under the cataracts of pain. But who put me into their bag? Isn't it a bit early to find myself crawling under the skins of the dying? Whoever is in charge of my training ought to be told to slow down. Dear Sirs, The honour you have conferred upon me cannot be gainsaid, but I am crushed and forgotten under its august folds. I am not ripe for this austere and mangy revelation. I am an unhallowed stripling in your silver halls. Oh believe me, sirs, it abashes me to stand in this land to which you have given me the rasping skeleton key. You see, my body is virtually unused, almost virgin, my eyes are fine, I carry but twenty-two years on my spinal cord. Hoping you will relent in apple-blossom time, etc.

Ah the tireless Chinese bliss of the traffic lights amazes me and puts me down. Flick. Flick. Flick. They never miss a beat. Heartless as the guy who pretends he's been through it all, they just keep tossing up those reds, greens, and oranges, while the night swirls around them and the desolation howls starvation in the face of the lamb, and I stand shivering on my bed of dreams, watching the stone walls of the buildings fill up with air.

Lord, now I think the time has come to say my prayers.

Prayer

Lord, let me see beyond my roundhouse, for I believe that something is there. Others have whispered that your void is crammed with light, and wasn't I born like them a small slippery bundle of crazy hopes? I am reaching out for your magic like a blind beggar-boy out on a hard night's ramble to earn pennies for his Daddy's falling whorehouse. Let me not mistake some breeze for your coin and smile too soon, and fool the department-store windows with frozen smiles. Lord, I cannot rest till I am delivered out of here. Lord, with the painfullest patience I am waiting to be batted clean out of the park into a new world that has no boundaries but the stopwatch you place around my pulse. But in the meantime, in the drag time, in the frozen time, in the wandering midnight cuckoo time, send me someone to talk to (or is that part of the test I'm in?).

Oops! I think I just said the wrong thing...
Scree-e-e-e-e-e-e-ch!

"Still here, eh? Merry Christmas, son."

"Same to you, Mum, but you know it isn't Christmas. It isn't even my birthday."

"Well, don't refuse a gift horse in the mouth. Have you lost all your manners, my poor angel?"

"I see you've got a new car."

"Yeah. Watch me floor it out of here. I can drag her all the way home to Tuxedo Crescent and back to this dump in 15 seconds. You'll still be here, I guess. I'll give you your present when I get back."

Ro-o-o-o-o-ar! Whoo-o-o-o-o-o-sh! ..1..2..3..4..5..6..7..8..9..10..11..12..13..14..15. Scree-e-e-e-e-e-ch! Bzzzz. Click!

"Pretty fast, Mum. Naturally I have no way of knowing—"

"—Ah still the carp in the soup, aren't you?"

"The fly in the ointment, Mum."

"Well, you certainly weren't put through a gentleman's home and brought up in that fine school to be a fly-in-the-night and a talk-of-the-town with your pants falling down and standing here on the corner till your shoes are worn out and building castles in the sand and barking at every floozy that passes."

"Cut it, Mum."

"I agree, let's not waste any more time. Here's your present."

"What is it? It's too cold to start unwrapping it out here in the snow."

"It's shoes, dear."

"Shoes?"

"Yes. Daddy's shoes. I stole them from under his bed while

he was sleeping. Why don't you step in here and try them on?"

"No, thanks. Here, you better put them back. He'll miss them."

"Please, dear, Don't pretend you don't need them. Why, you haven't a shoe to stand in. It takes all kinds of shoes to make a world and I'll just put another pair there instead. In the morning he won't know the difference. He's asleep."

"Thanks, Mum, but I'd rather not."

"Well, suit yourself, John—if you're going to be so difficult."

"No."

"What did you say, dear?"

"I said no."

"Why did you say that, dear?"

"My name isn't John. That's Daddy's name. I'm William."

"Oh all right, darling. Goodnight, my sweet little Timothy. See you next year."

Whooooosh!

Well, here I am, right back where I started from, wherever that was. Oh yes, probably much further back. Yet I was doing so well until I asked for someone to talk to. Now the blossom sky has fallen through the rusted spires of the old days and all I see are a few hollow, washed-out facts gathering together like refugees under the hopeless blasted skeletal umbrella trees.

Like all mothers, she exaggerates. First of all, my shoes are in perfect condition, or were the last time I examined them. Secondly, tonight is the first night on which I can record having been arrested by this corner, and I doubt if I've spent much more than an hour here. Nor is it part of my plans to be found stationed here when next year rolls around, or next Christmas, as she would put it.

It bugs me to have to go through all this. But what bugs me even more is that a few seconds ago I sneaked a glance at my shoes, just to make sure, and was sorely tempted to appeal to my watch and its ever-rolling calendar for a final verdict.

Is there no end? Will my holy inquisitors, who are not here, but are nonetheless hidden all over the body of the night, will my rescuers, whom I love and fear for what they once did, that I could not do alone, will they never stop discovering me in the same eternal jam and pointing me ways out that have long since turned phony and ephemeral in the dust parades?

They took me out of my mother's patchwork songs, that rang from her kitchen to every kooky cloister and back again. Oh yes, some time ago they led me by the hand out of my mother's stoked-up parlour car, that barrelled through every twist of the blizzard-ridden night, so old and swanky and condemned, and when the sounds died away, they all whispered "Here is the world: See? Now you're outside the windows, my friend." Yes, with all the pitiful strength of their arms they dragged me out of my mother's Mother Hubbard watchtower visions, so that they too could go on chasing the dreams that frightened them the most.

> Ah Judge! Judge! good-time Judge!
> Won't you shorten my pain?
> I don't like this lingering in the wings

Now it seems like indifferent news that my mother's songs have turned into a croak that makes the white acres of bathroom tiles look insane; or that the maid sits moping in the kitchen all day, and can't say why she hasn't even the strength to turn on the radio; or that Daddy can't find anything around the house anymore, unless my sisters show him; or that the school I was sent to, that Daddy and his father were sent to, has lost its name at last. It all seems so far away, because I'm living alone now. Yet I'm in prison all the same, and not one of my friends can tell me how I came here.

The slumkid is imprisoned in the threads of steam that drift from the wheeled hotdog stand, the countess is imprisoned on her velvet cushion, her husband on his polished saddle, the analyst is imprisoned in the fine print of textbooks by all the sick faces he knows he cannot heal, and convicts say they are imprisoned in the tiniest ray of mercy that shows in the bleak warden's eyes. I don't know the name of my prison, but I think it is compounded of all the failures hushed and buried in generations of success, and now all the silken bars are clanging so loud, I can't hear any of the messages from outside that might give me a moment's holiday.

"Well, sir, what takes you out into the cold, cold world tonight, in nothing but your imported satin pyjamas?"

"Duty, o street-cornered questioner. Duty. Nothing but duty. I am looking for my lost son. He is ugly. I do not like his face. He is all warts from ear to ear and how my wife can adore him so is beyond my comprehension. However, I am duty-bound to find him, for I wish him to know that his allowance has been cut for the third time in as many years."

"But, sir, this is a mission that will cost you dear. It has already cost you frozen ears; your moustache quite bunched-up with cold and the sheer glaze of your satin pyjamas are ghastly witnesses of your pain. The path of duty has led you into a cruel higgledy-piggle this evening. It has inveigled you to the very bottom of the winter, where your message has no more meaning than last autumn's kites. Sir, his allowance expired altogether some time ago, so why go on cutting it? Sir, your news is outdated and your son is fled. What more can I say but that I doubt if you will ever, ever find your son again?

"Not under the counters of dime-stores you won't find him, not under the covers of new air-tight plastic garbage cylinders, nor under the ancient battered ringing squirrel-delighting garbage tins that are passé but still keep their music going in the finest alleys of this city. Not under snow, white, black, or gray, in anybody's backyard, frontyard, or flowerpots. Not eaten with the snow in the snow-eater, nor blown with the snow in the snowblower. Not under pavement-cracks, nor under next year's rosebushes, don't hope to see his face. No sir. Your son is nowhere around, nowhere at all, but I swear to you by all the stars in the sea that he is alive and kicking."

"I am glad to hear that, o motionless Bleury St. talker. But is there really nothing I can do? Are all roads an empty snare? Will neither the wide white skid of Sherbrooke St. nor the worn-out snows of Bleury lead to my only lost son? Forgive me, but perhaps you have seen his footprint somewhere in the region dumps? He has a rather awkward stride, one foot being splayed and the other ingrown."

"No, I have never seen such a walker before, not even last night, when I saw everyone there is to see, and more."

Silence.

"Did you also see my wife, sir? Tell me—no one needs to know that we've talked, tell me—and let it be buried between us two strangers come together for a moment in the snow, tell me—and let it be but igloo talk the dark world will never know, whisper me just this one thing: what do you think of my wife?"

Pause.

"Well, she's not as pretty this year as she was last year, and she wasn't as pretty last year as she was the year before."
"Yes. And?"
"And so, through storm and sorrow, laughter and peace, through windshields and drain-pipes, through red lights and parties, life with its old sweet burden of wifely dreams, slides down the hill to the bargain basement where grandmas have their orgasms."
"True, sir. But you have not told me about my wife, *my* wife, my very own, who has unruly hair and big breasts and not a single freckle whereas I have hundreds, and who at this late hour, not so many miles from here, is lying in a warm bath, probably talking to her dogs and thinking of her children asleep upstairs all but one, her only splay-footed darling of a son. Is the picture not clear?"
"Yes."
"Now, sir, can we not dwell a moment on her character, the mystery of her ways?"
Silence.
"I can't, Daddy. Please go home."
"I can't go home. It's too much! It's just too much! Home is for sleep and work is for sleep and life is for sleep and I can't sleep a blessed minute. Duty keeps me up and she keeps me up all night with a million devices and the long sleep my grandfather promised evades me. I think I will go down to the river tonight and watch the ships that are frozen in ice. Oh stranger, poor cold creature who is no more fortunate than me, tell me now—only one thing remains that I really wish to know: Is there anything more beautiful than the wide wide river that flows past our city, flows around it and contains it in its great white frozen arms every long long winter since we are born? Is it not there that all our dreams are being answered, slowly, year after year, though we do not see it,

though we walk around looking at nothing in particular, imagining that we have forgotten them?

"Tonight I saw it from my house on the hill before setting out and I believe that was my real goal all the time, that was my reason for coming all this long way down, through the unforgiving ice and snow. . . .

"And now, good listener, since there is not a breath of wind to keep me here, and you do not seem ready to answer my question, I think I will be continuing on my way. Pardon me."

"Don't! Go home! Go home!"

"I can't now. It's too late. And I'm too tired to go climbing all that way again. My wife will be lying in the bathtub, still laughing perhaps, and occasionally reaching out to caress our two dogs, Bounder and Flounder, over the nose with a wet washrag. They are patient, forbearing brutes; and in any case the bathdoom door is locked, the key is turned on them and their miserable old habits. Oh they know by now, they know only too well that the odds arrayed against them will never change, yet they follow her into her bathroom every time they hear the water shouting into the tub. And now I think I can hear her laughter. The bath has gone cold, the dogs are tired to death of this game, but still she laughs with a laugh grown tired and old. Oh you may say it's only such a laugh as shakes the bellies of old organ-grinders, when they grind their organs too long for no reward, you may say. Or you may say she laughs like the sea in the bathtub of my house, and in it you hear all the crackling misery of the sea."

"Pardon me, sir, but could you say she laughs like the stars that are frozen so small in the window-panes of the sky— who laugh because they cannot live, and yet they cannot die?"

"Yes. And like the whole night that is weary of being called night when it has no name to go by."

"If so, the picture is clear, and in this laugh of yours you may count me a fellow-hearer."

"Good. Then it will not surprise you to know that I hear this laugh wherever I go, and have done so ever since I climbed out of the crib in my grandfather's nursery, and fell on the floor. Oh sir do not laugh. The sides of that crib were high, and it was a long hard climb and a gulp at the top, and a skyward glance and butterflies and diver's cramp, and then a flip and a roll and a spintail prance and a loop-the-loop and inverted dance and many a long caper before I landed on the poopdeck with my pants around my ears and my hands in hock."

"And what did your grandfather say?"

"He said: That'll teach him, the little varmint, to scorn the crib where my snow-bearded ancestors played—and now they're turning in their graves...."

"And what did your father say?"

"My father said: Yes, I suppose it will.

"And then my grandfather said: Will what?

"And my father said: Teach him.

"And my grandfather said: Teach who?

"And my father said: The little varmint.

"And my grandfather said: Oh ... oh, yes. Yes. that's the stuff!

"And my father said: What's the stuff?

"And my grandfather said: Son, you'll be a father yet."

"And what did your mother say?"

"She said: Aw, you men, you're all alike! Now will one of you please give me a light, instead of just standing there gawking at my poor darling who's gone and fallen asleep on the floor?"

"And what did you say?"

"I said: Get out of here, all you double-crossers, before I call the sheriff! I know it was you that robbed the stage!"

"And what happened then?"

"They laughed."

"Only they?"

"No. The stars, the dogs, the walls, the hobby-horses, bathtub, sky and sea. All the usual things."

Pause.

"And in what other times and outer spaces did you hear this laugh?"

"Must we go on?"

"No. please don't if you'd rather not."

"Well, perhaps I will go on anyway. . ."

His School Tale

The school was set on a hill, with woods behind, and a river around one side and running back through the trees like a hunted hare, and bold blue mountains seen far away from the dormitory windows. The cemetery, which served a village a mile off, that we were allowed to go and see twice a week on half-holidays, cascaded down one shoulder of the hill, and just before it stood the power-house where the kitchenmaids lived under all the electricity. In autumn and spring, when we had time, we used to watch them go past the school, from the power-house all the way to the kitchen under the old oak-pillared dining hall, and back; and in winter we watched them pass under the school via the tunnel. And any one of those times, if any of them looked at us, we believed she planned to waylay us some night with a word or a smile, and then seduce and torment us by slow infinitesimal degrees for all the bad hidden deep under our blazers, and afterwards tell the world and get fired.

And we would smoke in the cemetery, in the squash courts, in the woods, in the boiler rooms, in the ventilation shafts, in the damp, hot tunnel that smoked under all the buildings and windswept cloisters, by ourselves or with another who was happy to share in our weakness and bravado.

But how I paid for all that smoking in the long-distance runs! Ah how my legs ate the miles, the sweat-paved, the spinning, the silver and gold and rust-brown country miles, that soared away fuming into the distance at each turn, and how I thought I was doing so fine with a freight train somewhere behind hooting into my soul, and the streams saying "Yes, you have passed me," and all the autumn hills brilliant and glistening with the blood-drops shattered from my head and the sweat-parades streamed from my eyes, as I pounded the slopes so hard I thought I was done—and yet I would not slow.

But all the other boys were ages ahead all the time. Oh those solitary golden triumphs in the woods were nothing but a smoker's delight schemed from a smoker's weary turning brain. Yes smoker's hack was my downfall every ghostly minute, cutting my wind to a pittance, and all the miracles I achieved on that road were just the illusions of a lonely boiler-room smoker hunched over his weed and filled with weakness and bravado. So I knew when I reached my locker, spent and lashed half-crazy with despair, that the shadows of the boiler room were waiting, and had been waiting all that time, to take me into their lonely arms again.

My School Tale

Oh yes, sir. And the woods were so beautiful on the day

that I and my friend were sent out to cut canes. The paths rippled under our feet, as we waded through all the sun-shot leaves that were shattered on the ground. The paths led on and on, never ending anywhere that we could see or possibly hope to reach in the dim scarred remainder of an afternoon the supper-bells ached to close. Still, the trees sparked over us. Far over to our left the railway-tracks glinted through the maples and hill boulders, and down away somewhere on our right moved the river. And it was all so timeproof and still, I wanted to hold his hand, but he refused and said.

"Who are these canes for anyway?"

"Ourselves," I said, "you dummy, didn't you know?"

"Of course I know that. Who do you think I am anyway? I mean, who's going to cane us?"

"Most likely Pipi Leduc, the one and only southpaw swinger of the Prefect's crack-house."

"Say, how come he canes with his left arm and throws a football with his right and slings shit with his mouth?"

"Don't ask me. Maybe he canes with his left to save his football arm; then again, maybe he throws with his right to save his caning arm. For his mouth I can't speak just now. Oh don't ask me to track down all these mysteries. And if you want my opinion, I don't see any point in saying one further word at this juncture."

"What juncture?"

"This one, right in front of our eyes. It's the end of our woods, can't you see? We're not allowed to cross the railway-tracks without written permission, or unless we're running in the cross-country race—of bitter recall. If we're seen in the upper woods by the round Quartermaster with his hounds, you know what happens then?"

"Sure. Either the hairless Head will gate us, or our favourite Housemaster Jerry the Fairy, who shoots off under his chaplain's robes, will be after our rainbowed asses in a hurry—"

"—With all the stored vengeance of his shooting right arm, you might add."

"So here we are."

"Yes."

"When do you think they'll cane us?"

"After supper. Hardly will our supper be in our guts before it's in our upper abdomen again."

"Billy, are you afraid of being caned?"

"No. But I hate getting caned all the time like this."

"I don't believe you're not afraid."

"Well I never cry."

"Oh you just do like the others do. You freeze up so hard while you're waiting in line, you can't possibly cry, not even after six of the best."

"Maybe so. Because when Jerry the limey Fairy, who wears boxing-gloves in his sleep, when he laid in ten across my summer pyjamas and said he was sorry afterwards but it had to be done and 'You've got a lot of spunk, lad', then I cried all right. I couldn't talk for half an hour. And I couldn't even go downstairs to our favourite boiler room to hide, because it was after lights-out and the prefects on the floor were watching to see I went into the dorm."

"Yes, I heard you come in that night. You can't kid me any more."

"O.K., well I know you cried for mercy to Apple-Barrel Tex the Master of Cadets, he of the soft core, the floating belly, the primeval squad-car Santa Claus visions, before him you cried to be let off when everyone found out you were AWOL for the first blues parade because your buttons were all shone and your boots and spats a glossy black veneer but lo, your whole uniform disappeared at the last wink and you couldn't go up there in your underpants, could you, Jackie dear?"

"Ah but my cries were not in vain. I was let off."

"So what. You still cried."

"All right. But listen. Once I even heard Pipi Leduc cry. There he was standing in the basement bog, leaking and crying at the same time. He was moaning 'Mother dear, mother dear, I thought you knew, I thought you knew.' About what I never found out. But he sure did cry. He thought he was all alone, poor bastard; little did he know that I was sitting in the can right behind him, holding in my sides."

"It doesn't surprise me. They're all caners and complainers and feigners and insaners, and deceivers and believers, and short-changers and Christ-in-the-mangers, and thievers and grievers and coppers and teardroppers and liars and criers and doublecrossing priests. Why look at old Jerry. There were tears in his eye as he settled back into his wheel-chair all out of breath and told me I had spunk."

"Aw come on, now."

"What do you mean, come on? What about Greasy Dick, the history hick, who brands our bums with dates?"

"Come on, Billy, you're going a bit off the beam."

"Not at all. It's all there. You just have to look down and see. The year 2000 B.C. Written there. Enscrolled—clear as nightmare."

"O.K. I'll believe you."

"Good."

Silence.

"Jackie?"

"Yes."

"It's getting late. It's almost dark already. You can hear the wind on the rails."

"I know."

"Jackie?"
"Yes."
"We can't just come out here and cut canes and go straight back. It's too hard. It's too hard a life we have here."
"We haven't much time."
"I don't care. We'll run back afterwards."
"All the way? Who are you trying to kid? When did you ever win a race, pray tell, old Chief Smoking Log, old Tartar of the tarred and deathly lung, old seller of weeds and cancer in the woodland alleys, old smokefooted panhandler following your hot-rod down the hill, I can just see you caromming into the finish-line, fuming like the Federal Pen on fire. Ah listen you lonely, wistful thatch of smoke in the trees, when will the day ever come, that you can say, 'My smoking days are done. Now I can enter the brave races with all the other boys'?"
"O.K. Don't rub it in. Everyone knows I'm no racer. I never won a race in my life. Tho last year, as everyone knows, my sister won the sister's race."
"Yeah? I didn't know."
"Well she did. Walked right away with the trophy. But it was a mistake."
"How come?"
"My other sister won."
"Hey, Billy, what do you suppose your sisters are doing right now?"
"I don't know. I guess the runner-up's studying or walking or talking with my mother on Tuxedo Crescent. The other one, who got the cup, I don't know what she does with her time. She just lives over the ridge at Bromville Manor School with all the nuns."
"Come on, Billy, you know they're not nuns. They're ordinary Protestant schoolmistresses. Protestant. Like Luther.

Like Jerry. Like us."

"Listen, if I want to call them nuns, they're nuns, see?"

"Amen."

"Jackie?"

"Yes."

"I feel bad."

"So do I. I've felt bad all the time."

"Jackie, why do we have to go through all this? Why can't we just be men and forget it all? That's what this place is supposed to do, isn't it? Turn us into men? And scholars and gents and all the rest? Well, why hasn't it worked on us?"

"Don't ask me, but it sure hasn't."

"Then why are we still stuck in here? Why aren't we out on the streets with the rest of the world? Why aren't we out there enjoying ourselves the way other people do—pickpocketing and getting our pockets picked, and picking up the best dames and getting picked up for nothing by the cops and just having a good time while the money lasts?"

"Because it's safe in here. It's safer for us in here than out on the streets with the rest of the world. That's why, Billy."

"Oh Jackie, don't make me cry now. I can't go in to that prefect's room all soft and blown at the seams. We gotta learn to take it."

"Billy?"

"Yes."

"It's getting late."

"Oh I know. I can hardly see my hands. My feet are frozen. My eyes are up in the sky."

"And it's blowing hard."

"Yes, Jackie, listen to the wind! Listen to it tearing down the rails!"

"Let's go! We gotta run!"

"No! Not yet! Not yet!"

"Come on!"

"No! We're not going yet! They can't do this to us! I won't let them!"

"Billy, have you gone stark crazy? Touching me and mauling my pecker right in the middle of the path?"

"O.K. come on over here, then. Let's go!"

"All right, but we gotta make it fast!"

Crash! Stumble! Cr-r-ack!

"Owww!"

"What's wrong?"

"Billy, can't you leave go of me one second? You've landed me right in some thorns!"

"O.K. sit over here, then. Hurry!"

"All right! I'm getting there! Just sit tight."

"Here! Grab it, Jackie! Fast! I can't wait!"

"Take it easy, Billy. . . O.K. I'm there. I've got your number now."

"I've got yours better, you bastard."

"Think so, eh? You don't know anything at all."

"Oh no? See if I don't."

"You're nowhere, Billy. I'm getting tired. Hey, Billy-boy, what if I stopped?"

"Just try it, you little pecker!"

"I think I will."

"You bastard! Take that!" Slap! "And that!" Smack!

"Oww! Oww!. . . .O.K. Billy-boy, you've had it." Thump-thump! Scr-r-atch! Thump! Scr-r-atch! Thump-thump! Scr-r-atch! Scr-r-atch! Scr-r-r-r-r-r-atch!

"Owww! It sti-i-i-ngs!"

"Hey! Billy, you're forgetting about me now. Come on."

"Oh please, Jackie, don't! Don't stop!"

"Come on, then, get working, and I'll see about it."

Thump! Thump! Thump!

"Faster."
Thump-Thump-Thump-Thump-Thump!
"Come on, Billy, do something."
Thump-Thump! Squeeeeze. Thump-Thump! Squeeeeze. Scr-r-r-atch!
"That's it, Billy. Keep going."
"Please, Jackie, do me some more. Won't you even touch me?"
"In a minute. Just keep going."
"Oh Jackie, what do you want? What do you want?"
"Suck me, Billy-boy. . . Yeah, that's it. Harder, you old prick. Keep it up. O.K. now, bite, bite soft. Ah! Harder! Ahhhh! Scrape me! Scrape me!"
Mumble, mumble. . . "Please, Jackie. Do me some more."
"You asked for it." Scratch! Scratch! Scratch! Twist-Squeeze. Twist-Squeeze. Scr-r-r-r-atch!
Scrape-Slurp; Scrape-Slurp! Scr-r-r-r-ape!
"Ohh Bite me! Billy-boy, Bite me!"
Chomp Champ Chomp Scr-r-r-r-a-a-a-a-a-pe
Scr-r-r-r-r-a-a-a-a-tch
Yowwwwwwwwwwwwwww!
Yowwwwwwwwwwwwwww!
Squeeze Thump Squeeze Thump Squeeeeze
Slish Slosh Slish Slosh Slosh
Ahhhhhhhhhhhhhhh.
Silence.
"Oh God, we still haven't got the canes!"

And then it was brush, brush, brush to scrape the leaves off our clothes as we rose up spinning through the dark. And a shiver, shiver, slam! as the wind hit our spines and I slumped down crying, This is the end.

But oh no, Jackie tugs at clothes, Jackie "Come on!" grits

through frozen teeth, Jackie drags stiletto from a sheath and we move off cutting canes.

And crash stumble smash off the highway into trees, and Jackie: Come on stupid, over here! and all the poor drunks dozing at the wheel, and Jackie still: You nut I'm over here! And crack rip snackle snap, we break off canes, and whimper whimper bleeding hands again, and Oh God will this woods life never end? and Jackie: Just two more and then we'll scram. Come on come on, you're sitting down again. And out of this bathroom slumber shoots my pain, yes smoke has covered the bathroom door again, and the night-train comes and covers up my face, and Jackie: Come on smoky, join the race, get back in the human race, you sitdown clown. But my heart is with the poor folk underground, and us heartsick restless train-men leave no trace.

And Jackie: *One more cane* and then we'll run. I roll my eyes, Why run right into our pain? But Jackie screams: We'll get it anyway! He tugs my fallen shoulder, Get that cane! It's your turn now, you goof-off birthday queen.

. . . .So here we are, just picking birthday canes. And it's all right now, Jack, I'll go wherever you take me. But don't leave go, it's clear I won't make it alone.

But Jackie cries: You vegetable, this won't work! You got to learn to run on your own two feet.

And clickety-click, the canes are all under our arms. If you run right through, the night don't do no harm, and if Jackie pushes sideways from behind, I won't goof off in the bushes and come to harm.

But trippety-trip and a crash and all comes down. The canes, they all lie scattered on the ground, and Jackie lies like Fortune in my arms.

Oh the night won't know if we don't get up again. But Jackie: It's late. Let's go. Pick up those canes.

And then, my father, we're on the hoof once more. Running and crying like elephants through the snow.

And farewell, night. The bathrooms are all on show. And the dining hall lights cast downwards their iron shadow.

And Jackie:

Billy, Billy, Billy, stop crying. We've got to go in to supper.

* * *

Daddy's not here. He left without a word. He's gone like the streetcars, down the lonely cold tracks; and like my friend who fell in love with a streetcar and chased it into the river. He's gone like a sailor, back to my great-grandfather's clipper that lies buried under the harbour of some grey and smouldering town, that was old long before he slid in here to launch the Steamship Lines from his corrugated iron whiskers. He's gone like a matchstick drummer down the dark and candelabra'd halls of his mother's moan, and like a burnt parader in the Gobi, trailing one water-gourd and a skyfull of kites. He's gone like a clerk into the forests of his overlooked ledgers, and like a dancing frock-coated scribe, like a late dancing child of the dead spluttering Founder, into the blizzards of the Company's disregard.

And he's gone right through the laugh of his grandfather's Steamship Lines, and left all the bosses and secretaries to stare at the empty coatrack and laugh at their perennial void and touch knees under the table.

And he's left my sisters crying at the dining-room table, his doting changeless daughters who laughed as they sighed, "If we dust the sails on Great-grandaddy's clipper and take it down from the mantel, will you sail away with us tonight, Daddy dear?"—and he shouted, "No, silly girls!", and then laughed louder.

And he's left his wife who loved him, but kept turning the radio up & down, so he couldn't sleep with all the disaster-headlines soaring through his mind, so she sailed into the bathroom with her dogs and will be laughing there till dawn.

My father's gone and left me to shiver here alone like the Prodigal Son on the airfields of his choice—and only because he couldn't quite stomach my fairy-tale of the faraway school and the woods.

Now the burnt prophets buried under the pavement say he'll be back again with a last word before he heads for the river. (He can't go down there in phony silence, they murmur,—in a silence packed with tears and gastric disorders.) And I hope so too, but I really don't know what to believe.

Meantime the wind makes its rounds, the rails hum as they used to; and the stars overhead expect nobody in the next thousand years. The traffic-lights do not wane their fire, but I ceased to look at them long ago, I look at the white streets that lie like pregnant, forsaken angels, whole light-years from the gates they covet and remember. And they—they are silentest of all, they cannot speak, saliva drips from their mouths, their tongues are taken and doubled up with pain, they are caught in their dream like epileptics shivering in a fire, how can they tell me what this cracked old night will bring?

"Oh stranger, stranger, stranger, can't you give a poor nun a light when she's down and out?"

"I'm sorry, I don't have any ma—. Oh come on, Mum! what's with this nun's suit?"

"Never mind. I just want you to know I don't like the way you think of your father. So there!"

Pouf!

Oh the wind soars by, the tram-rails hum as they did an hour ago. . . but it's no use pretending. The old night has slipped and fallen down through the trap-door, down the cold and slippery stone steps it has taken a header into the cellar damp, and sees no way out; while upstairs, the people make no sound, they pretend they have no feet, no mouths, no ears!

"Pity bears the leaf. Pity slits its veins and lights the way. Pity is a mainliner through the night. Pity is the only redeemer."

"O is that your last word?"

Silence.

"Ahem! Ahem!"

"What? You here again in that horrible nun's suit? I see you've got a light, finally."

"Yes. The little man in the all-night cigar-store down at the corner was good enough to furnish me with a light. He then gave me a box of matches and said, 'Here, take this. It don't cost me nothin'.' And he added 'You look like a chain-smoker, ma'am, if you'll pardon the expression.' And yet I'm not a chain-smoker. I only intend to smoke this one foolish weed."

"Well, why don't you go home and smoke it, then, instead of hanging around here in that awful nun's suit?"

"I knew it, I knew it, I knew it."

"Knew what?"

"I've known it for years."

"What, for God's sake!"

"All this standing on the corner in the dark trying to build castles in the sand and staring at all the floozies' tails has finally got to your eyes. Your eyes are dim and worn like an old, old man's and, son, I hate to say this, but I fear blindness."

"What do you mean?"

"Perhaps if you come a little closer, you'll be able to see."

"What are you driving at?"

"Oh my poor darling, hasn't it registered yet? This is no nun's suit. These are widow's weeds. Your father died last winter, didn't you know?"

"O.K. That's enough now. I've heard enough. Just go home and do whatever you like. Smoke your weeds, if you like; and smoke your widow's weeds, if you don't like. Do anything at all. But don't come around here ever again."

"Oh all right—if that's the way you feel. We all have our casual ups and downs."

"Right."

"Well I guess I'll be getting along then. By the way, would you care for a lift anywhere? My car's parked just around the corner."

"No No No No! Get out of here! Go home and smoke your widow's weeds and die!"

Pouf! Zap! Pouf! Pouf!

"Pity is the only redeemer, my son."

Silence. 15-minute break.

Mother, finish leering at me from the bathtub or I'll come. Father, take your pencils out of my noonday hair. In the deserts of pity smart the hate-trees clean and tall. Pour all your hatred into my hand, old willow, and watch it turn my marrows gold. I have been to the mountains and the deserts and the plains. But the golden trams on Sundays punched my ticket to this bed.

O mother, lonely mother in the bathtub rolling, your salt thighs twined their Kyrie's around my brain. And lo, in other cities, other islands, I've blasted foreign women's mouths with rain.

My father sleeps like heaven in the frozen river. My mother's car just dances and forgets. My father willed a holster to my pocket. My mother, raven's eyes in alleyways. O listen to the bells on Patmos turning, the seagulls climb on pulleys through dark rain, the priests send all their vestments to the jackals, my mother's flesh comes storming through the glades.

Good housewives sip their Father's blood each morning, in the evening draw their skirts up to be saved, while landsmen moan their many-coloured warnings, and sailors to Madonnas leak their shades.

Good father, don't send money out to preachers on dark bridges. Their words are rags when winter has boxed your ears. A Saviour lies with his friends in the tall grass blowing. We two shall mount the almond-blossom hill.

The leaves lean out to children under night-trains. The doorbells cry upon a stairborne shade. Some stranger mother's rainy limbs will gleam and some day answer. But the night has already cut their cries from them.

The sand lifts knives in Abraham's second daydream. The darkling river thrusts away from him. Of all the frostbound sons who dreamed this murder, how many sensed that Abraham had no hands?

Automatons and bees shall be our saviours. The donkeys climb like cradles up the hills. The donkey-mothers mourn for their factory-children. And hungry Persian boys climb after them.

* * *

The saints shit up the ways of my Valentine. They think they can do no wrong, and I agree. When night falls down the hill, they'll still be squatting under the windows. Keep up the good work, old saints, we'll all get through.

I HAD NEVER NOTICED

The hornets in the woods call out for reasons. They wear black spectacles and point with their canes. Point on, old blackface, point past my shoulderblade, to where my family and yours lie stung in the glades. The streams sting their naked bodies, they lie all unmade.

* * *

Out of the woods come spinning twenty grandpas. And some are gamblers, but all ride bathroom staves. Their daughters turn to mothers like wind-charades. And into my infant eyes, all spin like brides.

Good sisters, you have cradles in your eyes. The storewindows swing the mercy-child like pain. A stranger to your bed brings peace like holly. But the noonday horses, the seadogs and I return.

"I Had Never Noticed" is the first section of a novel titled "Getting Through".

With But One Simple Step

MIKE FIORELLA

. . . rambling along the road hands shoved tight inpockets head enveloped in a fuzzy state of marijuana awareness hear the sharp grinding wail of pickup gears swelling from behind viciously popping the twilight balloon of silence bouncing overhead and suddenly from the nowhere a butterfly like a ghost, a monarch flutters to the ground weakly from over my shoulder dropping aimlessly and clumsily onto the grass right in front of me lying perfectly still just one instant suddenly making one long last miscalculated frogleap right into the middle of the road, mid August summer's almost over, fall then winter all the trees leafless and barkwhite, the ground snow-covered and frozen, everything'll look dead around here real soon, visions of the unseen California danced in my head like a Christmas dream, California where the sun always shines and butterflies never die, remembering gladly a cardreading lady I'd known once who revealed that in the tarot the butterfly is symbol of the soul, watching sadly as it floundered helplessly on the asphalt, no tender grassblades to cling to for rest falling awkwardly on the side of wing, unable to fly and so must die.

    Without looking back gauging time and distance by sound

ONE SIMPLE STEP

side-stepped onto the road cupping my hands as if to drink from them creating a tender trap for the monarch elusively hipping and hopping here and there on the road fluttering with an energy of desperate survival and in each flutter heard a plea, just a little more life that's all just a little more, crouched in chase like a groucho saviour trying to ensnare the winged insect acutely aware of the swollen scream behind me, jesus imagine gettin' run over killed trying to save a goddam butterfly that's gonna die in a few hours anyway a sure ticket into heaven, the gears singing now a new raw song of tires in third gear humming in the throat of the road getting closer now fast and the monarch just refuses to stand still and be saved, from what? from death to die that's what, even singsonging to it like a pet, here butterfly here butterfly, finally hipping when it should've proverbially hopped and fell dreamlike into my hands like a tossed coin in a blindman's cup and stood there and held it right there in the middle of the road examining its myriad swirls of mazelike color, the heavy shafts of breath from my nose disturbing the fine powdered coat protecting the veined wings tapping gently furious against my net of clasped fingers held almost in a pose of prayer, "poor poor butterfly" remembering when I used to hunt the Long Island ancestors of this particular creature capturing them gassing them mercilessly without trial in noxious deathsmelling hellman's jars mounting my trophies proudly in a frame up on my bedroom wall ashamed and sickened now at the littleboy joy I'd gotten out of killing living beings, my god how fuckin' long ago was *that*? Got cured though good and proper of killing, still young maybe only twelve when me and bestfriend Craig decided to skin a rabbit together that he'd shot the day before with his new birthday twentytwo. His mother and father weren't home and used an old dull carving knife from the kitchen and it turned out to be one hell of a bloody gut mess cause neither one of us knew what we were doing and sometimes hear now the sounds of rabbit flesh ripping under the dull pressure of the blade, an untrained stab, a rude tear of flesh up the soft furbelly, blood!, the dark beaded dead animal eyes watching us two boys perform our awful chore, no more guns no more knives please no more, the scream unbearably close now and almost absentmindedly step aside out of the way onto the grass letting my body roll into an oriental squat and gently pour the monarch from the cup and with a certain weary horror watch it flip its weightless body right back on the road, no!, proving only to be a nervous life movement of near death as it fluttered its way back just as unexpectedly to the safe green island of grass to do what it'd always been intended to do, die which isn't so bad when looked at as life in reverse gears, gears, and stood to glance up the road and there it was just making the curve, turning my back on it like it really wasn't there but instead find myself being stared down by one of those paranoid fantasies, really expecting one of these days out walking in the midwest sun for one of those screams to roll up behind me slowing down real easy-like a double barrel poking itself out the window and KA POW the kill a hippie freak for jesus scores another point the truck screaming up behind me now crawling right up my back like a wild bug flesh raising tiny fists of protest and just

ONE SIMPLE STEP

stood there really waiting for it defying the fantasy to become real, and am hit only with a bullet of hot air right into me right through me racing by harming nothing really except blowing around the scattered ragged bits of that popped balloon, still just standing there hands on hips watching and listening to the scream fade into a shriek a whistle a voice a low hum, gone.

Using an index finger like a windshield wiper run across my forehead, flick one last heavy fingerful of a day's sweat onto the road, snorting doglike at the new damp moldy smell of early country evening and shoot my arm up, palm out almost like a tv indian saying, how, in salute to my butterfly brother, "goodbye good luck die in peace" and leave him alone partly out of a respect for even this supposedly lesser creature and partly cause I don't favor watching anything die and start walking back to the house but after a few steps stop dead in my tracks strangely as I'd done once before on a cold winter rainstorm night months ago in Northpoint and considered killing myself, even acting it out right there in the two AM after hours street how I'd do it, molding my hand into an iron revolver placing the barrel in my mouth taking careful aim so the image bullet would not fail like an enemy lover but to burst through skullbone out the back of my head, and now stopping in just this same way all alone at the corner of a small back country crossroad where an open field grew wildflower, tall dry weed and could still hear the crackle of the day's heat in the high grass began to weep, not cry, but weep like the saints did, weep uncontrollably really regretting for the first time in my life ever every small stupid petty greedy humanact I'd ever committed, every unkind word evil thought whispered rumour and lie, every punch ever thrown in drunken rage every curse and insult ever spat out in anger every hurt ever caused upon others, parent lover or friend and really wanted in complete humility to forgive all those who'd ever hurt me, and I loved everyone, every single soul in the earth, people I'd never seen or would see, I loved them, and every living thing whether it flew on wings or grew from roots, whether it walked on two legs or a thousand or slithered on coldblooded bellies, I loved them and wished every one and living thing could just once see and feel the world, the universe thusly, so horribly meaningless life is seeming to lead nowhere but to death, but ah, how simply beautiful our lives like ocean waves determined to roll and tumble and froth unquestioningly, without hesitation from miles and tides away toward the inevitable unavoidable distant shore, how could any of us fear or be horrified by this one and only sure thing of our lives? And suddenly like when you're really involved in something and someone comes up from behind and scares the hell out of you, I almost jumped a mile when this pig farmer passes me by in a truck overloaded with squealing piglets, wondering what he probably must've been thinking under his strawhat, goddam hippie prob'ly on drugs!, and began to laugh just as uncontrollably at that feeling even love for this pig farmer who butchers his pigs squealing humanlike smelling death but are really laughing gloriously inside their pigsouls with the supreme knowledge that all butchering pig farmers come back to this world as pigs, realizing myself there is nothing really to be afraid of, nothing to fear, it all works out doesn't it, that the long journey ahead not only begins with but one simple step, but is itself the destination, that it'd taken me all my life to get just here right here on this obscure country road, that's what I've done that's what I do, and tomorrow someplace else, next week another and thanked myself for really not wanting to die just yet.

An excerpt from a long story

Morning Fragment With Dogs

STUART S. PETERFREUND

The alarm groans a six o'clock groan deep in its works. It has no hands, but is set to go off at eight, and is usually not more than a few minutes off. I am in between—between clock and pillow, day and night, dog and window: my mind has been slept in, is as rumpled as the sheets and the blankets.

The dog yawns, shakes itself, whines. It wants over me to the window. It wants the window open wider. I open the window, roll away from it, flatten myself. The dog sighs like something very old—furniture, a car, a house, a boat, a person, crawls over me to the window, pokes her nose out, extends a forepaw and elbow over the sill, and begins to navigate the house.

It is the dogs of the neighborhood that keep all the houses on course, at fixed distances from one another, moving at the same speed toward the same place as the sun passes overhead day after day. Some houses have more than one dog, and that accounts for how the houses without dogs are kept in position. The top dog

MORNING FRAGMENT WITH DOGS

in each house delegates responsibility for a dogless house, or if he is particularly fond of it, takes responsibility for keeping it in tow or on course himself. The system of collective navigation works: there has never been a mishap.

The dog sights along the east wall of the house, the first visible in the morning light, and calls out to the neighbor dogs, who answer back. Occasionally a cat joins in and is chided for its landlocked speech. Soon, a conversation of dogs joins the other early morning conversations. The dogs are a race of captains, of traders, of peak-capped, blue-overalled, pipe-smoking barge and canal men, with thickly reliable limbs, with thick red wives, silent, sturdy pale children. When they talk it is in Plattdeutsch, the language of fertile rivers and river estuaries, spoken by the water and by those who live on it. My breathing is the concertina that accompanies the simple dog-songs they set to work with. Freshly-washed laundry flaps from the rigging as we move toward a horizon that shimmers like beer or white wine, bearing the raw materials of that horizon: coal and ore and oil and grain and grapes.

The neighborhood depends on the services of the dogs. Without them, we would be adrift, at the mercy of forces and currents we cannot control. It is true the dogs must follow the current, but they keep control, keep course and position. Eventually, they must bring us and the rest of the cargo to a city. Cities are where we will begin a new existence under a new, more complicated set of rules. We have an idea of what the city is like, but because of the time, the idea will be very much different from what we had expected—older, more chaotic, large public buildings sounding the theme of anarchy encased in stone. We will become burghers and the dogs will not recognize us beneath the smells of frying and snuff and coaldust and bay rum. They will keep to their ways and drift on, until the only times we can remember the dogs and feel that everything is all right are in dreams and in distances, when the dogs talk across them.

Bourn

SAL YOUNG

Purty is usually good, today Purty was not he messed in the corner under the table which is against the wall away from windows from light a good place to hide. To go home after all that confusion finding home no one would believe it and I had no one to tell but Purty made coming home more unpleasant than I expected. "Bad dog!" I shut him in the closet in the darkness away from me I kicked the door a few times he would not stop yelping. I used to tell the neighbors the yelping was my ill wife confined to bed but they found out I did not have a wife or else she finally passed on, because I forgot one day when I had the flu and told Mr. Daniels the yelping was from backache causing nightmares; we are not allowed to keep animals. I am usually home there is nowhere for me to go I sneak Purty out in a shopping bag easily he is a little fat but not very long legged and likes the ride. Today he was mad at me for going out. It was the first time in two years I went so far and for many hours. Purty was mad at me he messed in the corner.

I yelled through the closet door at him "Compassion!" it has been a long day the sun is down I thought I would never get home Purty greeted me with tail wagging smiles back and forth as quickly as a flapping bird's wings so I thought to myself before my nostrils took in his disgrace and he remembered too. His tail shot between his legs faster than swearing a syllable.

Oh lord the things that will happen when I am not looking.

I had been yelled at all day yelling at Purty stunned us both silent. Then. I heard him plop down to the floor of the closet and pull his legs under himself getting old he could not find comfort—imagined that waxlike gray they, and maybe cats too, get under their eyes that is a mongrel's way of tears someone told me. I could not give in right away, no, beside myself I watched myself opening the closet door light bursting in salvation Purty glaring at my feet unforgiving this forgiver I was ready to ruffle his fur—please forgive me old fellow for I am ignorant and tired and friendships end every day but we are all we have left.

What could I say? A superstitious old fool like me who thinking about it cannot explain why messing in the corner is such a bad thing after all there is nothing in the Commandments about it. I tapped my knee for him to come. My conscience cringed as Purty rose his eyes all to knowing; I tapped my knee, his tail began the slow pendulum of a grandfather clock and he looked to me again like someone I should know from history who has returned to survey us. All ways in which we are neurotic this is one dead souls return to haunt the haunt. Napoleon? Newton? Churchill? The Babe? John Smith? John Brown? John the Apostle? John which was my father's name? A neighbor I never knew too well? Soul who took the bullet instead of me? Purty would not pant and acknowledge his true identity. Who will speak for me on Judgment Day? I am poor with words.

On this chair where there is barely enough room for my own comfort we are now both of us snuggled not trying not to doze as the huge orange of a moon rises across from my face through the window. I am glad I am awake to see this and home again. When I was too young to remember I was taught about time in a minute sixty seconds sixty minute hours sixty years longer until the lapse of worth I now know some minutes equal hours some nights longer than life can bear their seed years fleeting by.

So, who can tell? I have not been well aches compounding piling faster than unpaid bills in time the measure of space is the measure of groans or the relief from groaning. I am a comedy dancing to my own percussion ankles crack crack step by step those stairs worse than alarms, no burglars could ever steal into this house, we none of us can ever go out unnoticed, walls listening, this ancient place, those old boards creak along with me winter cold summer heat expanding contracting floors murmur in the nights of parading ghosts beyond the pillow over my head against the sounds of a symphony of age. Mrs. Crockett was out today squeaking away back and forth in her rocking chair on the warped chipped green porch big enough for only her, six milk boxes and me to squeeze through from the door pinned with clops of cotton there to perturb flies and bees. "You you you you you" she said, as if I were responsible for the two sheets tying her down to the chair. Unable to walk, I do not know where her daughters think she would run away to? I smile at her anyway I would never tie anyone down; I am a good neighbor. "Good morning, Mrs. Crockett" I said even though she probably did not hear me no one knows what she hears—some of the teenagers go by swearing at her unknowing their time will come if they are lucky enough to live such a long life. Or unlucky. I have not yet concluded.

"You!" she spit out. "You tell those children to be quiet!" There were no children. "Tell them to get away from here!" I listen. "I told them to tell those children but they didn't those bitches. You tell them!" Heave. Sigh.

She spoke her words out to the fantasia of dust wood chips sprinkling down from Mr. Pax's mop had gathered it all up was letting it all fall, the clanging stick against the iron railing overhead outside his workshop of wood carving kneeling praying children seven hours a day for Bible shops and elephant sales. The Internal Revenue will not discover this way of addition to his pension until he is dead and there will be, he explains, the famous discovery of his African teakwood "John the Baptist Head on a Plate" to make museums weep, but he would not have to worry about the taxes then when it is all said and done she was speaking to the hundreds of thousands of marigolds cramped together down the two blocks of grave-sized backyards held together by four foot high rusty brown fences crawling with rose bushes eaten by beetles speckled white by bird droppings over the years the sky indeterminable from April through September because of hundreds of dozens of laundry shirts, diapers, overalls and dainties hung from every pole and wall no other sight. A space of blue may not be sky, merely another apron background for the wood chips of Pax.

All was amplified by me in hot summer air, which dried laundry but drained my glands profusely. I was already exhausted by lead weights of sun, penetrated by the reek of marigolds, dizzied by the rocking of a rock of age. Mrs. Crockett, I would be senile too if I were you.

From the corner of my eye saw Purty with his nose against the screen snorting the breeze; pictured him standing on his hind legs human with paws on the sill waiting for that teeth-clenching screech of my passing through the gate. There remained nothing for him but the instinctual longing to get his teeth into marigolds and wrestle them out of the ground crunching dirt between his teeth pulling at them like he does my old socks, equal to the (dog) abandonment of (teeth) tearing up tissues—and revenge for another day alone. . . . Here and there the chirps of birds.

Oh Lord the things that will change when I am not looking.

I went out the back way, children play around front asking me to chase the balls they miss, laughing to hear my knees crack bending and reaching then throwing. Unable to bear their mocking I walked around the corner, crossed the street back to the front where Van Dyke Avenue has not changed since my youth. I had also waited on occasion for someone's grandfather to toss back, but I am no one's grand old man though they ask me anyway I suppose I love children but only when they are good, the same with adults, with myself.

So hot I could not recall why I went out but kept walking until finally it was too far to turn around in that heat unfit for anything but children, flowers and bugs,

cars on the way to pools I noticed sometimes. At intersections I forgot to look for traffic, was preoccupied by the tar bubbles up on the road the way they snapped when I stepped on them for moments unnoticing the burning macadam through my shoe bottoms like fire I could not wait for relieving white pavement again a gnat tried to fly into the corner of my eye.

Suddenly—I had not realized I had gone so far—those 942 steps to the bookstore where I worked for three years after I retired fearing all the while for my nerves. One day not wanting to think about what the day held for me, I counted how many steps there were from my front door to the store 942 steps foot in front of foot for a medium man at medium pace more in snow slightly less in rain. Today I was surprised at myself for not counting for once I begin counting anything I cannot stop: eye winks, breaths, cars passing, drips from the faucet; like a melody or slogan that will not quit running through my head. There was the day someone came into the store for an historical fiction; speaking with that person for an hour the whole rest of the day I could not put a foot down without thinking "John" next foot "Wilkes" next foot "Booth" next "John" next on and on oh Lord I thought I had better stop or I would be on that one again. Thought instead, today I did not count the 942 it must have been the thinking about Purty, no, the bugs, the sun the thoughts all the nerves I tried to swallow on the way to work I always kept telling myself . . . I will not let him defeat me. I will not let him conquer; standing staring out that window filled with so many colors books words signs, like standing over an area covered with autumn leaves beautiful, possibly symbolic, but hardly possessing when thinking about being home or something to eat, only a colorful mesh.

Then he was there, Ryan, seeing me but pretending not to in the manner so like him though yes better he would not acknowledge. My body stiffened to see him again. I thought better to move on. Could picture the way he would have slinked out saying "Well, Nexis baby, how's life dragging on for you? You sick, old man? Your color is poor, sweetheart." Every day it was the same thing if I was thirsty and took a little sip from my thermos in back of the counter he "Every time I look at you, baby, you're slurping away. I'm going to get you a camel's hump transplant so I can get some work out of you."

I walked those streets away from that store those thoughts to be active again felt good passing those houses with so much life going on carrying on

and on and on Ryan had needled me loving the thought of kicking me out of the job. However, even he was only a manager for the real owners were once acquaintances of mine and I suppose they hired me out of sympathy for I had a store of my own once not so stupid and not ungrateful I accepted their offer for work, not unpractical knew there is only so much hope to fill a stomach. My situation. I persisted. No matter what I could think of to say back Ryan would back right at me again not letting me handle anything but a dustrag.

Going around corners instead of going home, not yet with those nerves I had to work out or otherwise would take them out on Purty is neurotic I cannot even say no to him.

Ryan was sick, he had to be treating those students like blood brothers as if he were in on all the jokes and parties. He should have been an actor convinced eternal youth, though I heard his shoulders start to crack when he leaned over; saw him touch them in certain ways places—I dared not suppose; heard his cursing at me under his breath, for my age in time would be his; tried to ignore his wishing me—

"Baby, can't you think? Don't you have a brain in that skull or do you run on batteries?" Always more. Running his hand back through his premature all white hair "My son has a canary that uses its brain more than you, you know that? . . . I have to yell at you, you don't hear anything I say anyway, baby. Right? Right? Right?" It is all memorized in me all those hours waiting to die with me. I never looked him directly in the eyes as he went on, a plague at the back of my neck. "You thought I wanted those books picked out of stock to return to the publishers? Is that what you thought?" I never answered any answer would be wrong. "Are you crazy, Nexis baby? I've got a goldfish at home that's got more sense than you!"

Sometimes I thought he lived in a zoo; justice, it was the only thing kept me going. "You think you know what I'm thinking? Do me a favor. Don't think. All right, sweetheart? Don't do me the favor of thinking, it louses everything up." —The last shall be first. Oh Lord there had better be a heaven or there is going to be a revolution. I am a pacifist, but I would join.

Somewhere I had seen a clock through a laundromat window though I had forgotten the time it showed and how long ago I had passed it. I wandered by places looking so unlike places I thought I knew. No longer was there the Cozy Corner Cafe where the pie was homemade and free coffee came with a piece 40c where a vacant lot is now no one is fed there is more of everything this boyhood town of mine has grown.

When I asked for directions to Conroy Technical Institute on McDougherty Street, because I could find my way home from there, mouths dropped and one man stared "You sure you don't mean Conroy University on Truman Avenue?" I do not know much of this everything and less of anything recognizable. From my apartment windows I see some colored people occasionally as they pass, but there were many colored people standing around the Square. Only two years ago when I walked those same streets there was not a colored face to be seen; today even with so many no one seemed bothered by it is a mystery to me.

There is no Main Street anymore. I saw a sign reading Route 72 and the ladies muttered "On Fridays it is terrible to cross here" because of the car auctions outside of town which I remembered were always important. But Lord I used to be able to cross the street called Eisenhower Avenue once was Onawac Lane; Liberty Street is where Farley Street was and bless me there is Martin Luther King Court where once my brother and I ran to buy fresh eggs every Saturday before movies.

As the sun grew hotter I did not care if I dragged my jacket along on the pavement behind me. From my pocket I would take and eat peanuts I had bought from a fellow's stand in front of a bank some blocks past. To end all the walking in circles I went through a park to the sidewalk's end to a bus stop bench. There, as if they knew choice gossip about each other's secret disease, two women sat at opposite ends of the bench. Unable to strangle down a groan of relief I did not care and sat in the middle. Instantly both stood. I was the typhoid. They feigned an instinct about an imminent bus arrival by going to the curb and stretching their necks out to look away far away down the road. A policeman strolled over from the park asking about me. I do not doubt they had signaled him for I suppose I smelled badly, but their aroma of hundreds of minutes of bathoil hung behind them making me nauseous as the officer thoroughly looked me over. I walked with him to a squad car where he phoned headquarters and then offered me a ride "home." I thought that nice things are not always what they seem.

I stood baffled inside a convalescent home. The officer admonished "You shouldn't run off like that we have more things to do than chase after you the department tells me that this is the fifth time you've run away from this place they ain't going chasing after you again if you get into anymore fights over at Herm's Tavern it'll be your own tough luck you'll die without that medicine you know. What'll your family feel then? You going to put them through that misery?"

A young woman who did not know what she was doing came out of a door without looking at me her limp hand handing me a bedpan. I said "I don't understand what this is all about what is going on in this place is a mistake." Three women with canes one man swaddled in a sheet shuffled into the hall "Shut up!" I responded that I did not want jello or a hot bath or juice or to lie down all before the head nurse finally came out from wrapping gauze on the bedsores of a woman sadly dying from cancer. She explained I was not the man they were missing, no, not Harvey, he was still gone. Harvey was not like me she said he was a bit heavier with his big toe wrapped in a bandage and would have screamed them all out of there with his filthy language by now.

With apologies I was driven home some twenty turns this and that way never will I remember the way again. I went through the front door ignoring the shouts of the children as they in turn ignored the calls of their mothers to go inside. The steps squeaked one by one; I knew I was home with those noises so familiar Purty would probably recognize them as my noises too. I heard his paws scratching at the other side of the door waiting to jump up on me.

We rouse in the chair; my neck is stiff; Purty stretches his hind legs fall off my lap. All night we have slept here there is still time for a few more dreams. Purty off my lap will go over to the bed until it is time to get up for breakfast. I should not sleep sitting stiff for tomorrow there may be other places to go. The sun is beginning to dawn a certain joy I am glad I am awake to feel this and home. Harvey is not run away, but lost, I know. It is hard to count all the steps sometimes other things get in the way.

Bus

ALLAN LUKS

Walking with the table toward the delivery room, holding her hand. "Steve, I love you. Kiss me. Again." . . . Watching through the door's glass, the silence inside . . . then seeing the screaming from the red, curled wrinkles, the doctor turning to mouth to me: A GIRL. I smiled, a little laugh, "God, thank you." Me, everywhere inside, wrinkled, kicking, yelling, *now,* Me, yes!, wiping my eyes.

. . . In my office the next morning, sitting, watching, the softness sounding. Smiling. I stretched my arms forward, linked thumbs and threw this triangle straight over my head, straining elbows, shoulders, chest, neck—the air glob jumping out of my mouth, arms falling, laughing! Putting a finger in front of my mouth, "Quiet," I whispered.

Come on, stop it! Why should you get what you want? Who does?

Head manager of this restaurant. Supervise 90, their listening-watching me; and feeding-controlling more than 1,000 each day. People: "You manage *that* restaurant", and then questions.

My restaurant: finding possible locations, buildings, then market studies for each one, then shopping for banks, and their opinions, getting a lawyer. . . . No, I haven't really started, but I know—

If starting the restaurant . . . if this idea isn't me and for so long I haven't known it, then everything. . . . But then how could I admit it? The rhythm high in my thighs, sweet, fast, *no,* this is me. I do know.

. . . Waiting for the late afternoon bus to the hospital. Feeling the growing alongside, behind. Then the bus approaching, watching the sitting eyes tick by. Slowing, seeing the standing bodies compacted forward to the driver. Opening, "Take it easy, There's always another behind."

Inside, soft touching, then hard, squeezing shoulders, arms, hips, my groin too tight into a girdled ass, trying not to. *If they'd just change visiting hours, I could've left*—unbalanced stopping, doors folding open, hearing them inside and out, *If I had waited for the next bus—but I wouldn't. But it could have been one of those without—*

Someone suddenly rising, and I sat down. I looked through the window behind me at the flowing at this midtown corner. Starting. Now watching the standing before me, filling together. I saw her: the crumpled shopping bags inserted into each other like a puzzle, confused lint of gray hair ends, brown growths beneath her eyes, head shaking knowingly, expanded eyes watching everywhere. Sun's dots through the window hitting the back of my neck. I rose curled, then one arm straight up to grab a handle, and I looked into her eyes to nod, motion. She switched her bags to the other arm, began to push by several bodies toward the seat—

He popped out and slid into the seat, not seeing me, talking to his friend who had been sitting next to me. Their wrinkled suits and shirt collars bunched by tight tie knots, the gray hair. I reached down and touched his arm. His face hopped, growing eyes watching. "I'm sorry, but I got up to give the seat to this woman."

Looking at me, then rising—his friend's arm barred out, held him to the seat. "No, sit! There's too many damn people telling us what to do."

I watched his head which was now bobbing, seeing me, seeing everywhere.

Why her before him? Because there always has to exist a right way, so necessarily a first, second. And an awareness of it—from a sense?, learned? *And* so an awareness when denying this self. But if these two had to be feeling some part of this while they watched her and knew their thighs were stiff, nothing was moving—

Doors sighing open. Stepping, each holding-holding-holding the door for the person behind. Then I let go and started walking quickly to see my family.

From a novel-in-progress

Hunt

GARY LIVINGSTON

> *While I say* érèreh, *where can I take*
> *my child and go?*
> *Can I take it to the fields where there*
> *are no thorns?*
> *Can I take it to a bush where there*
> *are no hyenas?*
> *A field without thorns,*
> *where does it exist?*
>
> *—Gurage lullaby*

Watumi glare at staring sky. Not bad, elders say. Everyone too scared, too scared. Eyes like mouths, fast as hares. Watumi walk the Field now, proud as spear. Earth drink stalking sweat. Elders say all once this way; now loud insects to drown.

Watumi stop at little sounds, a change in grass, tell-tale murmuring. Some days the sky attack, but perfect now, against tense trees. Mostly open, swampy islands suck bare feet. Black fly try where bees went spent. Watumi stalk like plant, watch signs, ignore taboo and spreading welts. Cloth claws stealthy thighs. Bare chest reflects perfection of diamond. Burrs chafe ankles, dulled by nettles. Elders old enough to know, say, Go, see how the scarecrow grow.

Soggy log make sometime seat; rest come easy; Watumi sleep, delighting biting wings. Sweat sting eyes alert, great sun reclining. Watumi stir from dream of home. Dumb hunt, no food for drum. Scars haunt hedging grandsons, when world is done. Elders say began with too much gun. Lazy settlers, mocking water, ordering game. Mind less ways; hunt proper doctor, one who weighs life as a feather.

Watumi rise, follow rustle parting into mud. Good rain before leave footprints hiding beyond. Watumi bite dry jaws, clench spear for ready. Reeds come, blow down, cloud wind, hide homeward ticket. Eyes fight; elders say sleep come when won. Eyes slight; Watumi lean on gleaming spear that leave impression fading on forehead. Sun long unfinished yet, now mildly kinder. More frequent breeze distinctly river, brothers closer, older, chores with string. Watumi fish as boy, again to come. Now homeward, forward, farther than before. Many stirrings sway taut wrist. Stooping, listening back untwists; no passage here.

Brave trees hint. Shade insists. Watumi pursue eclipse, and why not prey? Thick roots entwine, umbra shelters pests. Enemies crawl for flesh, slapped dead, but more. Watumi rest each hotter step. Elders say one pay each way, no path is friend, though some might pray. The reed can bend, unbreaking, hiding guests or hushing invading footsteps.

Watumi freeze at every slender motion, impatient for

even failure. Elders say no way is wrong if all's intact. Murder's scar can char the soul, but only bile burns it. Watumi early learn his birth unearned, child yearned for mere perpetuation. Now he follow soon for all to know he knew. His woman, twelve, seduced unwily tourists with her hardships, crooked face unquenched by sex, boys destroyed by seventeen. Watumi had been through it secretly, and with success, his bride to be.

Sun withdraw behind brilliant wisp, slide out, scorch icy fringe. Watumi laugh, spear drunken leaning, little sun-tip shaking. Elders say alone, unknown, confronting unseen levels. Watumi cry, too tense, too tense, dense tests, old stars ajar and bones that build unfailing fence. Elders say enjoy the door if not its destination. There will be more, off polished corridors of timeless fortune. To chance, too much; Watumi gaze at sunset. Wind meek, reeds softer rubbing riddled with careless movement. Watumi halt, spear poised, neck bulging, shoulders ribbed with sinew. Marking rippling clue, Watumi breathe once hugely, watching waiting mossy break. First head, then body, long tail emerge, alert to threat; scurry to escape unpleasant clearing. Watumi hurl, spear sure, instinct ahead of ignorant maneuver, tip glinting dot, tilting down across New York mirage, impaling water rat.

It was

STANLEY NELSON

then
        Spencer   Lepon
Spencer, Spencer Lepon
it was the attendant, the one in the
cafeteria
behind the kitchen door (what mnemonic rites occur,
Katie, behind the kitchen door?)
                                Lepon-Lepon-Lepon, the
    notorious voodoist/voodoer
                                    later
for you
       Spencer Lepon
                I have seen you
asleep at the cafeteria table, I know you
from when
Victor picked you up in the schoolyard
                        but that was *wrong*/the wrong
Man
     only a darkman, and you are a
                       BLACKMAN
blacker than my father, who was, after all, only a little man
from Poland but when blackened by the hot Florida sun told to

sit in the back of the bus and he did
not caring that people thought he was
                                        black/Negro/Afro/colored or
what
       fine-boned and delicate
like you,
       Spencer Lepon, though he lacked
your haitian elusiveness, your giddy glissandic
glide as you glide along the stairs of my little house in
Brooklyn my little broken-down brownstone where I am safe and
secure surrounded by friendly Puerto Ricans   you are sliding
down my bannister with a stovepipe hat and a cruddy cigar
seeping through my house like a jungle orchid, drums
are beating all around you
you are muttering voodoo monosyllables *Leg-ba/Ban-bah-lah*
you pause at the third-floor landing for a spit-second snack of
                                chicken-wings and hot peanuts
then slip toward my bedroom   the door is ajar
my wife allcuddly in her naked morning sleep
then
       It was

then
       Spencer   Lepon

     you are taking out
              your Ogoubhatshal
              mywhatabigblack

     I digress, as usual

so right away to the Okra Tavern Rhonda is in from college for the Christmas holidays and she has discovered a *fabulous* joint in the East Village
    this was very long ago when hippies were still beatniks before the
time of afro haircuts when Negroes were called colored instead of black
      to top it off Rhonda is tall and thin with a strange Nordic blondness
despite her name that makes me think sometimes *Is this your daughter,*

IT WAS

Gideon? and every male with balls in the Okra young black intellectual tavern is plotting through his hornrims (for these were the faraway days before rimless glasses, obsolete predashiki days of the button-down collar) although the bar and backroom are dotted with white cute mostly redheads

we move uneasily, my wife and I, against the rhythm-and-blues, unliquidly, unnegroidly, to a table in the corner   Rhonda is penetrating the blackness by tilting her head at a casual nordic angle she developed from watching Swedish movies and we are nonchalantly ordering draft beer   *May*

I join you?   *he sits*   at the one empty chair in the Okra Tavern across from me between Rhonda and my wife   black as pitch, small as a girl, delicate Egyptian features with the erotic almond eyes, but he wears a fur cap like my father must have worn in bleakest Poland and his cheeks have a crystalline moisture like he has walked in snow flurries/it has

not been snowing

You have a lovely daughter   *He is talking to my wife*   **I am haitian. My name is Spencer Lepon. I can do voodoo magic—white magic, of course.**

Of course—my wife smiles. She likes Spencer; she thinks he is *cute*.
Spencer turns to me   **I can tell you all about yourself, Mr. Schiffer.**
Tell me.
You are a Gemini; your wife is Libra. Your wife's name is Elizabeth, people call her Betsy, she is not Jewish and she is from Indiana. Am I correct?
Correct.
You appear unmoved and unconvinced, Mr. Schiffer.
Rhonda taps him: **You can convince me, Mr. Lepon. You can do something for me. I want** *that* **one. Get him for me. Rhonda is pointing at a tall, muscular, Morrocan-looking youth who is standing at the bar in a white turban and kaftan gibbering in whatsoundslike Arabic**
Spencer Lepon nods and lights a roll-your-own cigarette   **I do that**

for you, sweetpea. Turn your head to the door
                              and shut your eyes
Shut
       Eyes   ouch   glint/I
               know you   Spencer Lepon   you are
Baron Samedi
             Lord of the Dead Souls of the Cemetery   and you are
the white-aproned attendant
who cleans the butts from the floor
of the all-night cafeteria
                     I have seen you mid mops and pails and
Soapsuds
           disappearing behind kitchen doors   *what do you do back
there*   *cooking under a dim red light*   *your batches of*
ox-gall powdered lizard jasmine and heliotrope crushed pineapple holly
leaves goat testicles beef heart sheep brain   tasting blood of the animals
and insect squashings
                     you have the stench of
                                          Sacrifice

What
       When
              Ok   Rhond   ra   a
and the Morrocan
                   occurred, he has materialized within the allotted time,
Spencer Lepon has made him occur, and he, the Morrocan, is standing
over Rhonda showing her a silver clasp and mouthing
panarabics and
            what's this   Spencer Lepon is looking at my wife
he doesn't blink   the whole rest of the bar is looking at Rhonda
but Spencer Lepon   looks at my wife   *he must know something*   he is touching her tiny plump fingers I love so much and he
notices her high cheekbones (cherokee) like his own and her semislanting
eyes
    I am telling your wife that I am a sculptor, Mr. Schiffer. My wife is En-
glish and she is now in England with my little girl. I am here to make con-

tacts in the artistic world. I am staying with Vergennés, my former mistress who taught me tapestry-weaving and who understands me. I used to teach in Rotterdam and I seek a similar position with an art department in one of your universities. I send messages to my wife in England.
 You are a family man, Mr. Lepon. You keep in touch.
 But I do not use a pen and paper, Mr. Schiffer. And I do not send telegrams or use the telephone.
 No?
 I send messages through my mind. I release messages into the astral ectoplasm and my wife receives them in England.
 Does she reply?
 Yes. But of course   *he smiles*   she must use the more conventional methods of communication. A Britisher cannot be expected to know voodoo magic   *the bastard charms/he turns to Rhonda*   How did you make out, sweetpea?
 Great. He's from Zagora, in the Atlas Mountains, a very remote area of Morocco. He doesn't speak much English, but we communicated. We exchanged phone numbers.
 You are a lovely girl. I wish you were my own daughter. *Spencer Lepon stands, puts on his coat and furcap*   I must be going. Vergennés is giving a party Saturday night for all us Haitian expatriates. Please come; this card has her address
 The card: an address on Bleeker Street   *look up* and Spencer Lepon has disappeared into the blackness, a little jungle man in an alien city
  but by the powers of the jukebox
  I swear I hear

boulou   bocice   segbo   libjah   voo
    doo   doo   willhoo

 in the cab to Bleeker Street my wife shows me photos of Spencer's sculpture   huge ancestral blobs   all black   black steel black   stone black wood   but *black*   bolou   bocice
 That man
       is talented, says Rhonda
who has not looked at a piece of sculpture since I took her hand and showed her those fake Etruscans in the Metropolitan but *what really hurts*

      my wife, who knows her art, says *Spencer*
   is a genius   *a genius*   **at what?**   so I pay
the cabbie his unreasonable fare and we make our way to Vergennés'
third floor walkup, a typical Saturday night in megalopolis, but what greets
us inside is not typical, but is
   darkness
                              candle
                                             a roomful of Haitians
all, for one reason or another, expatriate, having voodooed Duvalier (and
failed) or having plain decided to become *civilized*   albeit there is
nothing poor in this assemblage
   Indeed these tawny faces have an aristocratic cast and the basalt bodies
are clothed like the beautiful people   for we are in the days the longago
when blacks had not yet discovered   *blackness* **but had discovered**
Brooks Brothers/Florsheims/Bloomingdales/Saks   *but you cannot fool
me*   any adept can tell

any cabbalist who has leaned
his elbow on rough wooden Horn
and Hardart tables
and listened while Cousin Everett drank
hot tea with lemon and discoursed through icy winter nights, who heard
the Negro priest play Fats Waller organ arrangements in the Italian cathedral on Wyckoff Street
                                     could tell could tell these were
Zombies   mysteres   hou-gans/mam'bos   each riding his
particular
   Evil   cringing in her particular   Nemesis
although the dances takes the outer form of twist, meringue or mashed
potato, the real dance is occurring on a spring night in a haitian courtyard
under a large tree, the abode of Baron Samedi, the ceremony is invoked
by three drums and seven chants the mam'bo sprinkles water on the earth
of malodors and kisses the magic bell four zombies entering nude with
white painted faces are swaying and groaning and lifting black candles to
Papa Soho the commemorants are twisting the necks of young chickens

IT WAS

spilling the blood into earthen pots breaking the wings and feet and beaks drinking rum from a jug that is passed around filling pots with giblets, feathers, cornmeal, pigs feet, goat intestines, sausages, plantain, beans, tomatoes, sheep dung, bird tongues, ox bladders, lizard scales, castor oil, mushrooms, elm root, licorice, peanut butter, guinea-pepper, the powder of a decomposed corpse

and now begins the jumping, jerking, staggering, writhing, hopping, leaping, drumming, hammering eternally monotonous Batala oo   Batalla oo

Batala oo   Batala
                             oo   and in the magnetic
Center of the room
              near the wood-burning fireplace (it works, is lit) stands
                Vergennés
                       born Bernice Yankleovitch on a *shtetle* in Russia, but now the Mam'bo Miracia of the Bleeker Street scene, ageless Vergennés, the Jewish-Ethiopian nose and the Russo-Mongolian eyes set in fold upon fold, wrinkle upon wrinkle, but distributed in such a way that the woman could be 40, or 70, or a cataclysmic 35
                Vergennés
                wearing a simple apricot-colored robe and a Coptic cross
                surrounded by tapestries of her own making
most in the mythylogic mexican style with titles like Chicomecoatl Hunts Partridge" or "The Bath of Tezcatilopica," all, strangely, bordered by cutup Jewish prayer shawls and all, somehow, displaying a face that is
                Vergennés
                       the name taken from a small town in Northern Vermont
        RT.22
        Vergennes
                    the name seeming to meld with her predilection, at the time, for corrugated cartoons and fruit boxes
   a new carton and box collection by Vergennés will be displayed at
   the work that gained her a coterie of admirers, mostly gay, who wrote

incontrovertibly indecipherable articles about her genius and were stunned (but they forgave) her sudden turn from boxes to tapestries

    It was the shadow, explained Vergennés with a slight Russian accent. *I could no longer discover the interplay of the focus of light and shadow, and so concluded that light and shadow no longer exist/this being so, I could no longer look out my window, even though I wake up early in the morning, and so was impelled to discover that my walls were entirely bare—I had been fooling around with cartoons and boxes like a silly juggler—and my walls were crying out for*

  Tapestry

       Vergennés/Aide Wedo

                the name also seeming to meld with her new-found love for haitians, especially haitian men, especially haitian male artists like

  Spencer Lepon

                she took him in—this was very long ago—expatriate, and taught him lovemaking and tapestry-weaving (though he ended up a sculptor) and opened a gallery to display his works and those of other haitians and in returns he ran away and married an English secretary though Vergennés would always remain for him   The Woman   she would always have her choice of other haitians, many taller and more Africanly regal, but her heart cried out for *my tiny Egyptian*   **I have**

  told this all gestalted   **it never**

     could not have   **happened**

                just this way

  but immediately inside the apartment Rhonda has found Spencer, her arm is around his shoulder, she is whispering in his elfin ear   Spencer smiles   whispers back *Apolihsahgbadya* and again he materializes the Morrocan   spic-and-span in his turban and kaftan emerging from what is apparently the bathroom   he and Rhonda are quickly in a corner *communicating*   and just as suddenly we are in a circle sitting on straw mats and eating cheese fondue   myself and my wife and Vergennés the only white faces

    Spencer is next to my wife/cross legged and rolling a cigarette glittering in a many-colored Ethiopian vest   Vergennés is tolerant, aloof, she

IT WAS

  senses what is happening though I am engrossed in my cheese fondue
    she has borne much pain, Vergennés, from her little
    Egyptian
      Genius   It is my wife saying the word   Spencer has passed out
photographs reproductions of his sculpture/it is clear he seeks my wife's
approval who does indeed look petite and Cherokee in her simple black
dress   only *her* approval   the others are merely Zombies
    voodooed apparitions summoned by this wispy-bearded hou'gan
    to fill up the room/the Space   What
    do you think of my work, Betsy?   *Betsy already so familiar*
    You are a genius, Spencer Lepon.
    I taught him, say Vergennés.
    You taught him well, says Betsy, and Spencer
      Smiles
      he has voodoohoodooed
                        my wife Bolou Bocice
Batala oo
    I am undergoing a curious disorientation
priests and Victors and Cousin Everetts and Clarence Mios levitate before
me   apparitions   photographs
  flipped over become
                  darkness, a
                        negative
my head is throbbing something awful
the shadows of candles are huge and floating on the wall
encroaching the tapestries of Vergennés   /   and then I see
the astrally ectoplasmic
                spirits of Spencer Lepon and Betsy
                rise and fill the room
time is a microscopic slow-motion cinema track
each of their quietist gestures—the flicking of an ash, the
rolling of a cigarette, the touching of a fingertip—becomes
infinitely epic enlarged   suspended   heroic   as if
cockroaches suddenly became
                      Lions

      they are filling up *all the Space*
absorbing
   everything at the edge Segbah of
 Lisbah Vertigo
     Batala
       oo Batala

oo
  I am in bed in my pajamas *the light hurts my eyes*/**Rhonda and Betsy** are putting pillows under my head
  The light hurts my eyes
  We'll turn off the lights in a moment, darling. You had too much absinthe. We had to take you home.
  I had no absinthe. I've never had absinthe. I don't know what it tastes like or even looks like.
  You had plenty, daddy. Also I think they put hash in the fondue.
  Well, daughter, are you still impressed by Spencer Lepon?
  Rhonda smiles as she turns out the light **Mom likes him. I do too.** My Morrocan's name is Mustapha. Spencer found that out. Spencer knows everything—just about.

  Syllogism the word persists *Foreordained/Foundation Universe*
  for it was clear to me and has remained
  Clear
     that the concantenation of small events, some yet
     to be ordained, was welded to the Total
     Equation, and that Spencer Lepon had, like
     Edgar Cayce, become adept at contacting
     those Manichean particles that interface
     the world of real events and the Larger
     Reality that controls those
Events *you dig?* I had no hash or absinthe it was Spencer Lepon, the
     Syllogism
      Spencer Lepon
        wading in it,

                                                                    IT WAS
     absorbing and refining
                          It
                          piecing each piece
                                            together
                                                Seeing
the Swamp   the red-winged blackbirds   Cathedral   light/semi-
slanting Veritas/veritatum   autumn sunlight   my little sled   the
corset shop on Cortelyou Road   kaddish that became the sanctus
Fernandel-
    nosed laborers and the bocci court   Wurlitzer   Atlantis
    Stonehenge   this northward/Alien   City   in the
    Snow
         Spencer plys

                                                               how else
Explain
    my passivity when Spencer phones a week later
    I have decided, Mr. Schiffer, to accept your invitation to Thursday night
dinner.
    Oh, *What invitation*
    I leave for London next morning. I must wake up early. I will bring my
suitcase from Vergennés apartment
    Dinner   Parties   holiday
                        Season   the participants appear
and disintegrate, fluttering
in light, dissolving
            in darkness, everything
                                    melds into the other   And so
appears Thursday evening in my little brownstone Spencer Lepon,
Fern and Denny, young married friends of Rhonda, who is out for
the night with Mustapha, but Fern is black/colored/Negro
    though Denny is
                    Caucasian
                    and that was in the faraway time
when, if you invited one Negro, you invited *another,* and Fern
has never met a haitian

           Betsy
has prepared a beef bourguignon
                      and heavenly hash
which is not hash at all but a midwestern dessert composed of
fruit salad, whipped cream and small marshmallows (strange,
those midwesterners)
                  I am safe
                        at my diningroom table
                        in my little brownstone
                     I control
                       what happens here

   I did not spend my wedding night with my wife, says Spencer as he drinks his coffee and spoons his heavenly hash.
   You spent the night dancing around a boiling pot, messing with a voodoo recipe, says Fern.   *Fern doesn't like him*
   Spencer smiles   I spent my wedding night with Vergennés, my former mistress. The Schiffers have met Vergennés.
   I think you are making this up, says Betsy, who is wearing an apron and cleaning the table in housewifely
   I'm serious. I make things up only when I really want to. This really happened. Vergennés requested it. She has done so much for me; I could not refuse her.
   How did your wife respond to this minor request? *Denny is intrigued.*
   Hold on, says Fern. You're not learning any of this little man's voodoo magic. *Laughter*   *Jolly*
   My wife respected my feelings in this matter, as she does in most matters. That is why we have such a good and loving relationship.
   You're a little hou'gan, says Fern.
   Spencer laughs   I have my secrets.
   Dark ones.
   White *and* dark.
   How do you feel about negritude?
   I don't feel anything about negritude.
   You, a French-speaking Negro, should care especially about negritude. It was invented by Fanon, a French-speaking Negro.

I care about Spencertude. The rest of the world can care about negritude. Don't you identify with the black struggle? *black/not*
   Afro   Colored   Negro
May I remind you young lady that you are, like me, married to a white. The better to show my blackness.
I don't have to parade my blackness. It is there in my art. My art tells me what I am.
Then you should spend more time with your art and less time trying to seduce white chicks.
   Spencer laughs and rolls a cigarette   You are really obsessed with this black-white thing. The truth is, sweetpea, that I have no preference in the color of the women I seduce. I'll prove it: let's dance. With your permission, Denny?
   Sure.   But be careful.
                   So
this leads to a peaceful, domestic holiday scene; Denny and I
discussing the college basketball tournament; Betsy-in-her-apron
clearing the diningroom table; Fern and Spencer, politely it
seems, dancing in the kitchen to an FM station   when
   the scene
         very suddenly   shifts/blurs
Fern grabs her coat
from the closet, flings
Denny's coat at him (Denny)
and strides out the front
door into the
snow pulling her husband
behind her   and I swear I heard her say
                   Filthy little nigger
though Betsy denies it
            claiming that the two colored people
            had a heated argument about the then
            embryonic black power movement, but I
            still think it was because
            Spencer popped his balls against her

                        belly while they were dancing and
Spencer   he is nonplussed
                        he sits on the couch
rolls a cigarette
            pours another cup of coffee   and looks at Betsy
and looks at Betsy
            not suggestively, no, he's too self-controlled for
that, not possessively, no, but
                        premonitionally   as if he already
possessed her
            had voodooed her   I am tuned in but I do not show it
   I play it *cool,* man, Bogart style
                        like in the days
                                    of Clarence Mio
bocci   bocci
            they are talking *to each other* (I am
            left out) about people
                        I do not know
Spencer's people
            from Vergennés party
                        I do not remember meeting
It is clear that they are conversing
in a code language that Spencer has telepathized into Betsy's
unsuspecting mind—if only I had sent away for the magic decoding
ring that glows in the dark—for how can I accept the notion that
Spencer's uncle is an insurance salesman from Hempstead, Long
Island, or that his sister is married to a caterer from Hasbrouck
Heights, New Jersey but I say nothing, I do not interdict or
intercede
and anyway
            my head is throbbing again/I look at Spencer and see
My father
      fine boned
                  with a Syrian delicacy   *it must be*
the cigarettes he smokes

IT WAS

small darkman
            wearing Cossack boots and a furcap with bells, eating apples
and raisins and nuts and pomegranates, drinking
                                  hot Russian tea with lemon from
a glass
flying over winter
            rooftops Chagall-like
                        kissing the moon, breathing
stratospheric ice-air
            icedrops
                  hanging from his beard and eyebrows
as he glides into the
                Milky Way   a system a
       Syllogism
           the origins of the Slavs
are unknown and must, perhaps, remain hidden forever in the
dark night of time   Little of   their   early   beliefs   is
Known. **Awake. Morning. In my bed. In my bed next to my wife,**
Betsy. Betsy is asleep. Betsy is nude. I am in my pajamas. I sit up, put on my
slippers. Stand, put on my robe. Each move is accurate, exact, flowing into
the next move. A chessboard. Chess: Why did I go to bed? What time was
it? Why did I leave Spencer and Betsy alone? Forms. Fill out the forms. Go
to the principal's office. All my life. Well, I was cool. Fine morning. Sun-
light. Betsy
        wouldn't/No
           All's
              well
Betsy is nude in our cozy third floor bedroom   *I have gone down*
a circular staircase   **Rhonda's door is shut in her second floor**
back bedroom   *with sun in my eyes*   **and**
                                          Spencer Lepon
stands in fine winter sunlight
in the second floor frontroom, his bed
already made up, already shaved
and neatly dressed, smoking one of his

strange cigarettes, his leather suitcase
packed and snapped   I am beaming   *life is good; everything
in its place*   **Spencer**
  Smiles: May I join you for coffee?   *a good guy after all*
  Fine with me; only I've got to rush. Working man, you know.
  Of course, Mr. Schiffer. Don't trouble yourself. I'll prepare the coffee.
    nice domestic scene, me lathering up, Spencer fixing
coffee,   only
          where there is Spencer there is
Strangeness
he has somehow found our wedding pictures
and, as he hands me my coffee, he says: These were on the table,
Mr. Schiffer. *Since when?* Were they taken in a church garden?
  No that's a temple.
  Yes, I thought so, It looks a bit like my grandfather's temple.
  Your grandfather . . . ?
  I am really Jewish, Mr. Schiffer. My grandfather was Chief Rabbi of Haiti.
But my father converted to catholocism when he married my mother. Many
members of my family have remained Jewish—My uncle from Hempstead,
for example—the one you met—still practices the dietary laws. Your wife
looks quite lovely in her wedding gown. I will put these back.

  Yes   possible/possible   all is   a little blackman in a Cossack cap
could have emerged from the steppes
   of outer Mongolia, as well as   jungles of Ethiopia   and the Jews
wandered   a common root perhaps   perhaps the Lapps
   whose blood type has not been identified   or the Samoyeds of whom
ethnologists claim a common ancestry with the Mongols,
   Negroes and Caucasians
the circular staircase
         Sunlight
              harsh
                 wintry
                     to third fl   ouch
I swear
   I saw

IT WAS

        Spencer
           It was
              Spencer Lepon
I saw his black *poteau-miten*/**saw him**
shutting   shutting
            the bedroom door   where Betsy
lies nude
  Repeat/SlowMo/Camera Track/Repeat/Slow
  He knocked at the door and told me good-bye; that is all, Gideon
  but
     I swear I saw his Ogoubhatshal/leaving
the bedroom
       the door is ajar   he shuts   ouch/glint
sunlight
  my eyes   his nostrils turn inward and he becomes
first a green goat
         and then a red bull   *bolou bocice*
         and finally
            batalla oo
       grimacing god in a striped polo shirt
battered stovepipe hat   cruddy cigar
                  Legba

It was Rhonda he really wanted—did you check the second floor?
Women—how devious

                    Legba
Master of the Crossroads   he knocked
  at the door and told me good-bye; that is all,

Gideon
Bolou   **geometric separation of the**
               cabbalistic matter represented
               by the ritual water

Bocice   **which produces the magic**

                    possibilities of the visible
                    phenomenon
Battala   practical consolidation or
                    centralization of the dispersed
                    powers of
oo   astral space geocentric
                    utilization of the stellar
                    atmosphere

Ategbinimose   Odanbhalah   Wedo   Dangbe
Recurs. I create my own aeons, my own pleromas. Spencer creates his own aeons, his own pleromas. Spencer and I and my father, may he rest in peace. It recurs in winter, in sunlight, in my little Brooklyn brownstone, on a third-floor landing when the door is ajar every morning   It is a prayer
                            my body speaks   And there is nothing left to tell
     except that once I saw Vergennés
in a Brooklyn supermarket, and I was surprised to see Vergennés either in Brooklyn or in a supermarket, and especially in a pants suit sans her coptic cross, so I speak:
    Good morning, Vergennés.
Who?
    Vergennés.   I know you as Vergennés.
    I am Bernice Yankleovitch, young man. I have always been Bernice Yankleovitch. Mind your manners and your tongue.

The Universe is Not for Sale

HARRY SMITH

THE UNIVERSE IS NOT FOR SALE

: A voice within Gawaine startled him. *Shit,* he cut himself. *Stupid*

THOUGHTS WHILE SHAVING

, like an item in a bad newspaper column, announced—*announced* (*yes!*) in a voice much like his own but not his own. *No! Not mine . . . thinner, faster, efficient,* more efficient; *Message* spoken as fast as perfect clarity allowed, the clipped urgent tone of a *newscaster. Yes,* a voice *different* from any of his familiar ways of speaking, much different from his usual heard-thought.

Monad. Goddamn monad. He snickered.

:*Stupid.* He examined the nick on the bottom of his chin—not bleeding much. He joyed in splashing cold water on his face. The voice had helped him to *wake* up, he thought; he had been *Half-Asleep,* he decided, feeling a sense of significance, of discovery, as he realized that he sometimes arose so groggy that he continued his dreams even while shaving or showering. Hearing the voice had been something like that,—*A Voice From Sleep*.

Gawaine strapped on his watch, 8:55, rushed to bedroom, began to dress quickly.

"Daddy! Daddy!"—Gareth yelling imperiously in the hall.

"Yeah?"

"Hurry up. It's Late. Mom says you should Hurry Up!" the boy announced, entering. Elaine followed: "Bad boy, Daddy," she shouted, and giggled loudly.

"OK OK, go put on your coats."

"What are you doing up there?" Ruth called, as the children were descending the stairs.

"I'm coming!" He finished tying his shoes, draped a tie around his neck (*Tie it later*)—the tie lying out from yesterday atop the jacket tossed on the big bedroom chair. "I'm coming!" He grabbed the coat, ran putting it on hurrying downstairs. As he was donning his overcoat in the lower hallway, Ruth snarled, "You drive us all crazy when we can't get you up in the morning."

He nodded sympathetically, kissed her on the cheek perfunctorily—"Goodbye."

"*Goodbye,*" she said.

He opened the door as he picked up his manuscript-bulging briefcase that he had placed there the night before. Outside, on the brownstone steps, Elaine told him, with an air of cleverness, "You drive me crazy, Daddy."

And the children ran ahead, skipping, and waited for him at the corner, and after the crossing they scampered ahead again the half block to the nursery school, and he saw the morning sun and the sunbrown of Gareth's hair and the golden & red-glinting curls of Elaine, and he thought them fair; and soon, after all the almost unthinking helloes to children & parents, he was away, in the Court Street cafeteria.

THE UNIVERSE

The first sip of his coffee was a molten pain whelming from an upper front tooth—the one just left of center, he decided, *Goddamn dentist.*

Gawaine had submitted to the perils of the dentist's chair only three months earlier. *Perverts. Loving fingers in mouths.* His dislike of dentists exceeded even his aversion to barbers. *Irrational. Oropervo! Pain-lover-fuckers.* He suspected his dentist who always complimented him on his endurance of pain of deliberately inflicting great pain instead of advising injections. With his tongue, he felt the tooth, sounded the cavity, *first on front of tooth.* The second sip of coffee hurt much less. The orange juice had not hurt, he supposed, because it had been cold & the tooth cold. The third sip of coffee hurt very little. He relaxed.

As usual, he had bought *THE NEW YORK TIMES* before entering, but today he did not wish to read yet; he would read it in the office. He listened to the massed voice of the cafeteria babbling—a pleasant, friendly murmuring, unlike the quick stridency of coffee shops or the muttering bellicosity of bars.

Why THE UNIVERSE IS NOT FOR SALE?

Salesmanship?—A momentary confusion, then Gawaine remembered the concerns he had taken to bed: schedules & sales, production details & business discussions, advertising & letters & promotion—yes, all the minor necessitities of action impending (*necessities?* necessities *Only* for *mundane efficiency* in the *system* of *work*): *small:*

THE UNIVERSE IS NOT FOR SALE

: a way of reminding himself of the pettiness of such matters, he theorized. *Buying & selling*: Buying & selling should be rela-

225

tively unimportant in a life.—Yes, *The Joys of Life NOT FOR SALE*:

"The best things in life are free,"
he sang in his mind.

: Monetary success is no true measure of a man. Money should be only a *means* toward reasonable ends.

moongo We moongo   *pulled*
-pushed to & fro   *pulled*
to & fro
      & pushed & worn pushed&pulled & worn by motions before us & beyond us, Inevitable as moonpull
Inevitable
moonpull
      the wear of spaceforce
Down Down

weight & time

flesh stress virus mould & old & old
                        Nitrocarbo
                                  -hydro
       lalala

                Lavoris for the Clitoris
                Keeps you kissing sweet

       lalaLa

The bridge: rightness. Walking *Right* a bridge, *to be on a bridge* the great bridge spanning his neighborhoods, home & office; from community, elm & brownstone, from humanscale to Manhattan skyscale—unplanned complexes, thrustings, aspiring urgent ugliness near in the cold clarity of brilliant winter morning, all so high and yet so small against the vastness of the sky.

THE UNIVERSE

Like a crusader's destination
Momently, Gawaine saw himself as a crusader
:
forth
each morning, over the bridge, to assault each day anew; forth over the bridge from the courtly garden of his life onto the Towering World.

Entrepreneurs/robber barons of business and even culture
business culture
robber barons & their vassals
: sly merchants lawyers literateers:
The Saracens, in granite bastions.

Assault Saracens Strongholds Enemy?
—*Ego metaphor, healthy ego,*
he mocked himself: *easy too easy* Easy to see corporation rulers Saracens, with base minions. **Con Ed.** *Easy:* Con Ed, the sleazy churl, slithered to power called noble. Craven shrewdness. Manipulation of weakness. *Always private profit before the public good.* The Great Blackout was a miracle of private enterprise.

metaphor too simple metaphor. emotionally satisfying
 CHEW WRIGGLY FOR ORAL SATISFACTION
 CHEW YOUR LITTLE TROUBLES AWAY

Thus, with a moderate feeling of self-satisfaction, perhaps tinged with smugness, Gawaine set forth for Manhattan. He was glad he had time to walk over the Brooklyn Bridge. Especially since the subway strike when he had walked routinely, he was always loath to ride the subway.

Soon, he was on the bridge. Ahead, beyond the massive grace of the stone arches, Manhattan—the structures of rampant will, *like a crusader's destination,* the words of his friend Abbe.

Only a solitary stroller before him, walking fast, soon out of sight. After the days of the subway strike when the bridge pedestrian walk had been thousands-trafficked, it seemed strange that it was almost deserted. The Squibb building neon sign flashed 27°, milder than yesterday; and again, bright sun, the sky pure robin-egg blue. It felt good to be walking, seeing in the brisk morning.

Nets – steel cords upward like raised nets taut

Below, the dark blue of the harbor, rippling at incoming tide

Tide tide pull & flow
moongo moongo

Moongo; cycles independent of all will

the tides, the orbits, a woman's phases

I know, I know, the poor fools.
         In most lives,
the highest dreams are expressed bizarrely as in the skyscrapers with grandeur in their ugliness. *The world the world, a world I never made*
           Grandeur in ugliness
—the early skyscrapers such as the Woolworth building before him *(yes)* the granite-sheated ascendency crowned by a mock Gothic spire *Onward & Upward* religion of technology,
—today the irreverant *cold cubes,* the stark *powerliths*

Only the few—the dreamstrong Empire State soaring . . . graceful strength; The gold-burnished building of Mies Van der Roe . . . One the few—

O the bizarre the sad the lives, the sadness of most lives.

And I?

THE UNIVERSE

Better? Innately better?—Rhetorical, long, long being with his question: What is the greatest genius but exercising more of the potential human intelligence? *Every child born with a healthy mind ...*

And who are you
                     to say otherwise?

You noble liar! coward! hero murderer saviour fiend, my friend, you clod & Keats! You banker petty thief derelict farmer pervert priest: What were you what might you what are you what will you be?

Rich man poor man beggar man thief
                             : "*Chance.*"
                     Determined
by factors impossible to vector: "Accident" : complex: *Unknown*

And every child ... O God the children

Every child. *History!* History is the evidence.
*Who could tell? Lincoln Edison Napoleon Einstein—
Who could tell?*

*Achieve: the only measure the must of measure: Action:
Creation. Find, find the perspective the freedom,
the freedom for the greatness*
                     Know Thyself.
Most men are in slavery to events, enchained by conventions and compelled by misunderstood desires. *Objects of desire. Condition Conditioned.*

To know the nature of desire, the composition of conventions, the causes of events
                —Freedom is the recognition of necessity
  – Engels

      Tolstoi Epicurus Christ Spinoza Farrell Melville
Swans. Two swans.
       Signs, not swans.
White signs in the water near the shore. Warning of *shoals? No Trespassing?* White long-stemmed signs upon dark blue water. *Like*-sized, some likeness of shape: like-formed *whites on water:* an expectation of swans.

Gawaine felt physical relief. *Strange,* why should there be physical relief? Soon, he recognized the cause, – relief from the strain of weighty thoughts. He smiled. He had been tensing muscles as though his entire organism were alerted to a direct survival challenge.
           thought/survival
– a wonderful organism.

Red white & blue! America the smokestacks! The red white & blue smokestacks of the Brooklyn Navy Yard upshore, spewing great gray smokestreams. Involuntarily, he sniffed. He smelled the engine fumes & frictioned rubber, from the roadway below, and the faint salt breeze faintly rotten.
    People on the go
    Oubiedo Sunoco

People moved, dying in their filth. World
        could be a garden
and Gawaine dreamed divine buildings—mile-high, cloudhigh, with spacious gardens between each building, and the buildings grouped severally in loose clusters, wide parks between, and true countryside once more between the cities

Quick light footsteps behind
    probably a girl. Yes. She passed

dimples. fair/windpinked. darkbrown hair, browndark eyes

THE UNIVERSE

–and slimly ample. He noticed the slowness of his gait. With many short, strong steps, he increased his speed to match hers – *ideal* about 30 feet
ahead   She, tall & straight,

effortless grace   Wearing boots   *hunting*   lithe *healthy huntress*   – a wonderful organism

      objects of desire
He puffed slightly. Could he outrun her if they raced? He imagined her beauty, racing nude

      scrawled across plaque
          RESTORATION of the bridge
–Strong, his back & arms, his legs: he became exuberantly aware of his animal powers. Stared for the lines of her ass & thighs, but the coat was a trifle too loose to define her form [by elegant intention?] *chaste. Chase? Ridiculous* he slowed, and she was soon far ahead.

She began to disappear
                    bridge end.
downward   underpass
into the earth.   stairs

abyss

Dis

Sweat on his brow despite the cool. Coughs, racking *stop smoking*. He lit a Camel, coughed almost retched, bent forward. *gall* taste, then deep-inhaled smoke, sharp, and felt better.

Off the bridge. The girl gone.

Ahead, Printing House Square. Big Ben Franklin, the bronze statue given by the city to the printers of New York. Printing House Square? No printers there. The turreted old Tribune building, vacant, for the wreckers:
BROOKLYN BRIDGE SOUTHEAST   RENEWAL

As Gawaine neared his workday, last night's worry assailed him anew, intensified.

Hunted, he felt hunted.

from Gawaine Greene, *a sunken novel*

NORMANDALE COMMUNITY COLLEGE
LIBRARY
9700 FRANCE AVENUE SOUTH
BLOOMINGTON MN 55431-4399